'...and that's when it fell off in my hand.'

Further
fabbitty-fab confessions of
Georgia Nicolson

Confessions of Georgia Nicolson:

Angus, Thongs and Full-Frontal Snogging

'It's OK, I'm wearing really big knickers!'

'Knocked out by my nunga-nungas.'

'Dancing in my nuddy-pants!'

'...and that's when it fell off in my hand.'

'..then he ate my boy entrancers.'

Also available on tape and CD:

'...and that's when it fell off in my hand.'

'...then he ate my boy entrancers.'

'... and that's when it fell off in my hand.'

Further fabbitty-fab confessions of Georgia Nicolson

Louise Rennison

HarperCollins *Children's Books*

Find out more about Georgia at
www.georgianicolson.com

This edition produced for The Book People Ltd,
Hall Wood Avenue, Haydock, St Helens WA11 9UL

First published in Great Britain in hardback by HarperCollins *Children's Books* in 2004
First published in Great Britain in paperback by HarperCollins *Children's Books* in 2005
HarperCollins *Children's Books* is a division of HarperCollins*Publishers* Ltd,
77-85 Fulham Palace Road, Hammersmith, London W6 8JB

The HarperCollins *Children's Books* website address is
www.harpercollinschildrensbooks.co.uk

ISBN-13 978-0-00-776962-9
ISBN-10 0-00-776962-8

Printed and bound in England by
Clays Ltd, St Ives plc

This work of near geniosity is dedicated to my family: Mutti, Vati, Soshie, John, Eduardo delfonso, Hons, Libbs, Millie, Arrow, Jolly and the chickens. Especial love and sympathy to Kimbo and I am sorry about the enormous nunga-nunga gene. Gidday to the Kiwi-a-gogo branch, and greetings, earthlings, to the Isle of Wight mob. Big LUUUURVE to my mates even though I sometimes feel they do not appreciate the genius wot I am. Philippa Mary Hop Pringle, Jools and the Mogul, Jimjams, Elton, Jeddbox, Jo Good(ish), Lozzer, Dear Geoff (but it's huge) Thompson, Alan D., Gypsy Dave, Kim and Sandy, Downietrousers and his lovely wife, Mrs H and partner, MizzMorgan, Phil (don't, well I won't) Knight and his fabby Viking bride, Ruth, The Cock and family, Rosie, Sheila, Barbara, Christine and all the Ace Crew from Parklands. Love to Chris (the organ) and to Dezzer the Vicar and young Phil and all of the merry band of St Nicolas. To Baggy Aggiss and Jenny and Simon and of course Candy, to the Hewlings with love. Love to Black Dog and a special plea: please can I have a go at the joystick. Please. Loads of love and gratitude to Clare and Gillon.

And a special thanks to HarperCollins, now my worldwide family, with big kisses to Gillie and Sally in the UK and an especial thank you to the remarkable Alix Reid. Thanks also to the very talented team in the US... Finally muchos thankus to the thousands of really groovy and fab (if somewhat insane) types who have written to me and told me how much they like my books. Goodbye. Oh no, just a minute, thank you to everyone who bought *Dancing in my Nuddy-Pants* and made it #1 on the *New York Times* bestseller list. How groovy is that? It means I can swank around with my award at parties and so on. Although I have to say it's not easy wearing a necklace that is a fourteen-pound pyramid on a chain. But hey, that is the price of fame. (Or you might say it's the price of stupidity as the award is meant to stand on a shelf and isn't really a necklace.)

A Note from Georgia

Dear Chumettes,

Bonsoir!!! I am writing to you from my "imagination den" (or my bed as some people call it), just to say how much I hope you like "...and that's when it fell off in my hand." Interestingly, the Hamburger-a-gogo types (who I suspect may be a button short of a cardigan) called my book "Away Laughing on a Fast Camel". They said that "...and that's when it fell off in my hand." sounds too rude.

They are indeed weird, but what you have to take into account is that they don't really speak English as such. For instance "fag" only means homosexualist in their land. It doesn't mean cigarette. So when I wrote that "Alison Bummer lit up a fag", they said they thought that was "kind of cruel" because they thought she was setting fire to a gay person. I think that illustrates what I am up against.

Anyway, my little chums, I have spent many happy minutes... er... hours writing this and there were a lot of other things I could have been doing, believe me. Juan and Carlos – my imaginary maidservants – could have spent time amusing me, but I said (in my mind), "No, Juan and Carlos! Put down your guitars! Stop plucking! I must write another book for my lovely fans."

That is how much I love you all.

A LOT.

I do.

I am not exaggerating.

I LOVE YOU ALL.

Georgia xxxxxxx

p.s. But I am not on the turn.

Alone, all aloney, on my owney

Saturday March 5th
11:00 a.m. as the crow flies

Grey skies, grey cluds, grey knickers.

I can't believe my knickers are grey, but it is typico of my life. My mutti put my white lacy knickers in the wash with Vati's voluminous black shorts and now they are grey.

If there was a medal for craposity in the mutti department, she would win it hands down.

I am once again wandering lonely as a clud through this Vale of Tears.

I wish there was someone I could duff up but I have no one to blame. Except God, and although He is everywhere at once, He is also invisible. (Also, the last person who tried to duff God up was Satan, and he ended up standing on his head in poo with hot swords up his bum-oley.)

11:20 a.m.

This is my fabulous life: the Sex God left for Whakatane last month and he has taken my heart with him.

11:25 a.m.

Not literally, of course, otherwise there would be a big hole in my nunga-nungas.

11:28 a.m.

And also I would be dead. Which quite frankly would be a blessing in disguise.

12:00 p.m.

It is soooo boring being brokenhearted. My eyes look like little piggie eyes from crying. Which makes my nose look ginormous.

Still, at least I am a lurker-free zone. Although with my luck there will be a lurker explosion any minute.

Alison Bummer once had a double yolker on her neck; she had a big spot and it had a baby spot growing on top of it.

I'll probably get that.

12:05 p.m.

Phoned my very bestest pally, Jas.

"Jas, it's me."

"What?"

"Jas, you don't sound very pleased to hear from me."

"Well... I would be, but it's only five minutes since you last phoned and Tom is just telling me about this thing you can do. You go off into the forest and—"

"This hasn't got anything to do with badgers, has it?"

"Well... no, not exactly, it's a wilderness course and you learn how to make fire and so on."

Oh great balls of *merde* here we go, off into the land of the terminally insane, i.e. Jasland. I said as patiently as I could because I am usually nice(ish) to the disadvantaged, "You are going off on a course to learn how to make fire?"

"Yes, exciting, eh?"

"Why do you have to go on a course to learn how to open a box of matches?"

"You can't use matches."

"Why not?"

"Because it's a wilderness course."

"No, wrong, Jas, it's a crap course where people are too mean to give you any matches."

She did that sighing business.

"Look, Georgia, I know you're upset about Robbie going off to Kiwi-a-gogo land."

"I am."

"And you not having a boyfriend or anything."

"Yes, well..."

"And, you know, being all lonely, with no one to really care about you."

"Yes, all right Jas, I know all th—"

"And the days stretching ahead of you without any meaning and—"

"Jas, shut up."

"I'm only trying to say that—"

"That is not shutting up, Jas. It is going on and on."

She got all huffy and Jasish.

"I must go now. Tom has got some knots to show me."

I was in the middle of saying, "Yes I bet he has..." in an ironic and *très amusant* way when she brutally put the phone down.

12:30 p.m.

Alone, all aloney.

On my owney.

The house is empty, too. Everyone is out at Grandad's for lunch.

I was nearly made to go until I pointed out that I am in mourning and unable to eat anything because of my heartbreak.

Mine is a pathetico tale that would make anyone who had a heart weep, but that does not include Vati. He said he would gladly leave me behind because talking to me made him realise the fun he had had when he accidentally fell into the open sewers in India.

1:15 p.m.

Looking out of my bedroom window. Entombed in my room for ever. Like in that book, *The Prisoner of Brenda*, or whatever it's called.

Except I could go out if I wanted.

But I don't want to.

I may never go out again.

Ever.

1:30 p.m.

This is boring. I've been cooped up for about a million years.

What time is it?

Phoned Jas.

"Jas?"

"Oh God."

"What time is it?"

"What?"

"Why are you saying 'what'? I merely asked you a civil question."

"Why don't you look at your own clock?"

"Jas, have you noticed I am very, very upset and that my life is over? Have you noticed that?"

"Yes I have, because you have been on the phone telling me every five minutes for a month."

"Well, I am soo sorry if it's too much trouble to tell your very bestest pal the time. Perhaps my eyes are too swollen from tears to see the clock."

"Well are they?"

"Yes."

"Well how come you could see to dial my number?"

Mrs Huffy Knickers was so unreasonable.

"Anyway, I'm not your bestest pal any more, Nauseating P. Green is your bestest pal now that you rescued her from the clutches of the Bummer twins."

I slammed down the phone.

Brilliant. Sex Godless and now friend to P. Green, that well-known human goldfish.

Sacré bloody *bleu* and triple *merde*.

And poo.

Oh Robbie, how could you leave me and go off to the other (incredibly crap) side of the world? What has Kiwi-a-gogo land got that I haven't? Besides forty million sheep.

I think I'll play the tape he gave me again. It's all I have left to remind me of him and our love. That will never die.

2:20 p.m.

Good grief, now I am really depressed. His song about Van Gogh, "Oh No, It's Me Again", has to be one of the most depressing songs ever written.

2:30 p.m.

Second only to track four, "Swim Free", about a dolphin that gets caught in a fishing net, and every time we eat a tuna sandwich we're eating Sammy the dolphin. Fortunately I never eat tuna, as Mum mostly stocks up on Jammy Dodgers and there is definitely nothing that was ever alive in them.

2:35 p.m.
If I am brutally honest, which I try to be, the only fly in the ointmosity of the Sex God was that he could be a bit on the serious side. Always raving on about the environment and so on. Actually, his whole family is obsessed with vegetables. Let's face it, his brother Tom (otherwise known as Hunky) has chosen one to be his girlfriend!

Hahahahahaha. That's a really good joke about Jas that I will never tell her but secretly think of when she flicks her fringe about or shows me her Rambler's badge.

I will never forget Robbie, though. The way he used to nibble my lips. He will always be Nip Libbler Extraordinaire.

2:50 p.m.
Oh no, hang on. The Sex God used to snog my ears. It was Dave the Laugh who enticed me into the ways of nip libbling. Which reminds me. I wonder why he hasn't phoned me?

Did I remember to tell him that I was thinking about letting him be my unserious boyfriend?

I should punish him, really. It was, after all, he who introduced me to the Cosmic Horn when I was happy just having the Particular Horn for the Sex God.

2:55 p.m.
Phoned Rosie.

"RoRo."

"*Bonsoir.*"

"I am having the cosmic droop."

"Well, fear not, my pally, because I have *le* plan *de la* genius."

"What is it, and does it involve the police?"

Rosie laughed in a not-very-reassuring way if you like the sound of sane laughter. She said, "I'm having a party for Sven's return from Swedenland next Saturday."

"What kind of party is it going to be?"

"Teenage werewolf."

"Oh no."

"Oh yes."

"Good grief."

"Bless you."

"Rosie, what has Sven been doing while he's been away, working for Santa Claus on a reindeer farm?"

"He hasn't been to Lapland."

"How can you be sure? Geoggers is not your best subject, is it?"

"Well, excuse me if I'm right, but it isn't yours either, Gee. You missed out the whole of Germany on your world map."

"Easily done."

"Not when you're copying from the atlas. Anyway, I must go. I have a costume to make. See you at Stalag 14 on Monday."

Bathroom
3:00 p.m.
Sometimes I amaze myself with my courageosity. Even though I have been through the mangle of love and beyond, I can still be bothered to cleanse and tone.

3:30 p.m.
But the effort of a high-quality beauty regime has made me exhausted. I am going to go to my room and read my

book on my inner dolphin or whatever it's called. Anyway it is to do with peace and so on. I may even make a little shrine to Robbie to celebrate our undying love. Even though he hasn't bothered to write to me since he went to Kiwi-a-gogo land.

3:45 p.m.

Hmm. I have covered all the cosmic options with my shrine: I've put a photo of Robbie in the middle of some shiny paper, it has a figure of Buddha on one side of the beloved Sex God, and one of Jesus and a little dish for offerings on the other. Also, when I was accidentally going through Mum's knicker drawer, I found some incense stuff. I don't like to think what she and Vati do with it: some horrific snogging ritual they learned in Katmandu or something.

3:50 p.m.

I had to BluTack Jesus on to my dressing table because Libby has been using him as a boyfriend for scuba-diving Barbie and one of his feet is missing.

4:00 p.m.

Phoned Rosie.

"RoRo, explain this if you can with your wisdomosity. I only had the Particular Horn for SG before I met Dave the Laugh and then Dave the Laugh lured me into the web of the General and Cosmic Horns."

RoRo said, "He's groovy, isn't he, Dave the Laugh?"

"Yeah... sort of."

"Shall I ask him on Saturday?"

"It doesn't matter to me, because I am eschewing him with a firm hand."

"A nod is as good as a wink to a blind badger."

What in the name of Miss Wilson's moustache is she talking about?

My bedroom, in my bed of pain (quite literally)
10:00 p.m.

Libby's bottom is bloody freezing. If I didn't know better, I'd say she'd been sitting in a bucket of frozen mackerel. Still, she has been round to Grandad's, so anything could have happened; he is, after all, the man who set fire to himself with his own pipe.

10:05 p.m.

She might have a cold botty and be mad as a snake, but she looks so lovely when she's asleep and she is my little sister. I really love her. I kissed her on her forehead and without opening her eyes she slapped me and said, "Cheeky monkey." I don't know what goes on in her head. (Thank God.)

10:15 p.m.

Do the Prat Poodles deliberately wait until I'm drifting off before they start their yowling fest? What is the matter with them? Have they been startled by a vole?

I looked out the window. Mr and Mrs Next Door have put a kennel outside in the garden for the Prat Poodles, but the poodley twits are too stupid and frightened to go into it. They are barking at it and running away from it. How pathetic is that? It's only a kennel, you fools. What kind of dog is frightened of a kennel?

10:20 p.m.

Oh, I get it!! Angus is in their kennel. I just saw his huge paw come out and biff one of the Prat Poodles on the snout. Supercat strikes again!!!

Hahahaha and ha di hahaha, he is a *très très amusant* cat. He has set up a little cat flatlet in the Prats' kennel. It's his pied-à-terre. Or his paw-de-terre.

10:25 p.m.
Uh-oh. Mr Next Door is on the warpath. Surely it must be against the laws of humanity to sell pyjamas like his. He looks like a striped hippopotamus, only not so attractive and svelte.

He's trying to poke Angus out with a stick. Good luck, Mr Hippo.

Angus thinks it's the stick game. He LIKES being prodded with a stick, it reminds him of his Scottish roots. Next thing is, he will get hold of it and start wrestling with Mr Next Door to try to get it away from him.

10:28 p.m.
Yes, yes, he's clamped on the end! Mr Next Door will never get him off by shaking it around. He will be there going round and round the garden for the rest of his life.

10:33 p.m.

Sometimes for a laugh Angus lets go of the stick and Mr Next Door crashes backwards. Then Angus strolls over and gets hold of the stick again. I could watch all night long... uh-oh, Mr Next Door has seen me. He is indicating that he would like me to step downstairs. Although I think shouting and saying "bugger" at this time of night is a bit unneighbourly.

Honestly, I am like a part-time game warden and careworker for the elderly mad. I should get a net and a badge.

Mr Next Door's garden
10:40 p.m.

Mr Next Door was sensationally red as he tried to shake Angus off the end of his stick.

He said, in between wheezing and coughing, "This thing is demented, it should be put down!!"

Oh yeah, fat chance – Angus nearly had the vet's arm off the last time he was in surgery. The vet has asked us to not come back again.

However, I used my natural talents of diplomosity with

♥ 23

Mr Mad. I spoke clearly and loudly. "You need another broom to beat him off with."

I said again, "YOU NEED ANOTHER BROOM TO BEAT HIM OFF WITH."

He said, "There's no need to shout, I'm not deaf."

And I said, "Pardon?"

Which is an excellent display of humourosity in anyone's book. Except Mr Mad's. In the end, I lassoed Angus with the clothesline and dragged him home and locked him in the airing cupboard. Dad's "smalls" (not) will be in tatters by morning, but you can't have everything.

Sunday March 6th

Dreamed about the Sex God and our marriage. It was really groovy and gorgey. I wore a long white veil, and when I was at the altar SG pushed it back and said, "Why... Georgia, you're beautiful." And I didn't go cross-eyed or speak in a stupid German accent. I even remembered to put my tongue at the back of my teeth to stop my nostrils flaring when I smiled. The church was packed with loads of friends, and everyone looked nice and relatively normal. Even Vati had shaved the tiny badger off his chin, and Uncle Eddie had a hat on so that he didn't look quite so much like a boiled egg in a suit.

The choir was singing "Isn't She Lovely?" and for some reason the choir was made up of chipmunks and Libby was in charge of them. It was sweet, even if the singing was a bit high-pitched.

And then the vicar said, "Is there anyone here who knows of any reason why these two should not be joined in matrimony?"

I was gazing into the dark blue of Sex God's eyes, dreamy dreamy. Then from the back, Jackie Bummer (smoking a fag) shouted, "I've got a reason: Georgia has got extreme red-bottomosity."

And Alison Bummer (smoking two fags) joined in, "Yeah, and the Cosmic Horn."

And I could feel myself getting hotter and hotter, and I couldn't breathe. I woke up crying out to find Libby sitting on my nungas with Charlie Horse and singing, "Smelly the elepan bagged her trunk and said goodguy to the circus."

8:15 a.m.

It's only 8:15 a.m. On Sunday. I want to sleep for ever and ever and never wake up to life as a red-bottomed spinster.

8:30 a.m.

Maybe if I make a special plea to Baby Jesus for clemency, he will hear me. If I promise to put my red bottom aside with a firm hand, he might send the SG back to me.

8:35 a.m.

I can't pray here – Baby Jesus won't be able to hear a thing above Libby's singing. Maybe I should make the supreme sacrifice and go to God's house. Call-me-Arnold the vicar would be beside himself with joy; he would probably prepare a fatted whatsit... pensioner.

9:05 a.m.

What should I wear for church? Keep it simple and reverential, I think.

9:36 a.m.

My false eyelashes are fab.

9:37 a.m.

Maybe I shouldn't wear them, though, because it might give the wrong impression. It might imply that I'm a bit superficial. I'll take them off.

9:38 a.m.

It has taken me ages to stick them on, though. Anyway, if God can read your every thought because of his impotence ability, He will know that I really want to wear my eyelashes and have only taken them off in case He didn't like them. They didn't have false eyelashes in ye olde Godde tymes so it is a moot point.

Perhaps He will think they are my real ones.

9:40 a.m.

But that would make Him not an impotent all-wise God, that would make Him a really dim God. Who can't even tell the difference between real and false eyelashes, even though He has been watching someone put them on for the last half an hour.

And I say that with all reverencosity.

Anyway, surely He is looking at the starving millions, not sneaking around in my bedroom.

In the loo
9:50 a.m.
Is He watching me now? Erlack.

In the street outside my house
10:10 a.m.
Quiet, apart from Mr and Mrs Across the Road's house. As I passed by, there was loads of shouting and yowling. I hope Mr Across the Road is not ill-treating Angus's children. He looks like a kittykat abuser to me. And he has a very volatile temperament. The least thing sets him off. He's like my vati. He appeared shouting and yelling at his kitchen door as I went by to God's house. At first I thought he was wearing a fur coat and hat until I realised the coat and hat were moving. He was completely covered in Angus's offspring.

Naomi as usual is not taking a blind bit of notice. She is a bit of a slutty mother: mostly she just lolls around in the kitchen window enticing Angus with her bottom antics.

Last week the kittykats, who are ADORABLE, if a bit on the bonkers side, burrowed their way under the fence and were larking around in Mr and Mrs Next Door's ornamental pond.

I said to Mutti, "I didn't know the Next Doors had flying fish in their pond."

And she said, "They haven't."

The flying fish turned out to be goldfish that the kittykats were biffing about in the air. When the mad old next-door loons noticed and came raging out of the house, the kittykats cleared off back under the fence. I don't know what the fuss is about: they got the boring old goldfish back into the pond. Even the one caught in the hedge. Anyway, as punishment, the kitties were caged up in the rabbit run. Not for long it seems.

Mr Across the Road was trying to get the kittykats off him, but they had dug their claws in. They are sooo clever.

He shouted at me, "They're going, you know. They are going."

Rave on, rave on. I bet he loves them really.

Church

Call-me-Arnold was alarmingly glad to see me. He kept calling me his child. Which I am clearly not. My vati is an embarrassment in the extreme, but he is not an albino. Call-me-Arnold is so blondy that his head is practically transparent.

I really gave up the will to carry on when Call-me-Arnold got his guitar out to sing some incredibly crap song about the seasons. Why can't we just sing something depressing like we do at school and get on with it? I even had to shake hands with people. But I must remember this is God's house and also that I am asking for a cosmic favour.

At the end, after most people had filed out, I noticed that some people were going to a side chapel and lighting a candle and then praying.

That must be the cosmic request shop. Fab! I would go light a candle and plead for mine and Robbie's love.

I went up and got my candle and lit it, ready for action, but an elderly lady was kneeling right in front of the display thing. I could hear her mumbling. She had a headscarf on. On and on she went, mumble mumble. Bit greedy, really. She must have had a whole list of stuff to ask for.

Ho hum, pig's bum.

I knelt down behind her because I was feeling a bit exhausted. I had, after all, been up since the crack of dawn. (Well, eight fifteen.)

I was holding my candle and thinking and thinking about the Sex God and our love that knew no bounds and stretched across the Pacific Ocean. Or was it the Australian Bite? Anyway, our love was stretching across some big watery thing.

I think I might actually have nodded off for a little zizz, because I came round to see a small inferno ablaze in front of me. Oh hell's teeth, I had accidentally set fire to an elderly pensioner! The end of her headscarf was blazing merrily and she hadn't even noticed.

I started beating the flames out with my handbag. I was trying to help, but she started hitting me back with her handbag. Before I knew it, I was in a handbag fight.

11:45 a.m.
I did try to point out that long dangly scarves on the very elderly could be considered a health hazard around naked flames. But Call-me-Arnold wasn't calling me his child any more and he didn't ask if he would see me next week.

Which he won't.

Lunchtime
I am exhausted by trying to get along with the Lord.

Monday March 7th
Back to Stalag 14

As a mark of my widowosity, I wore dark glasses and a black armband. Also I found a black feather from Mutti's sad feather boa that she wears if I don't spot her first. I stuck that in the side of my beret, which I pulled down right over my ears.

I was walking along with Jas and I said, "Even in the depths of my sadnosity I think I have a touch of the Jacqueline Onassis about me."

She said, "Why? Did she look like a prat as well?"

A quick duffing up showed her the error of her ways.

Oh God, oh Goddy God God, a whole day of Stalag 14.

Assembly

Our revered and amazingly porky Headmistress Slim rambled on about exams and achievement and said wisely, "Now, in conclusion, girls, I would say, it's not all about winning, it's how you play the game."

What game? What in the name of Ethelred the Unready's pantyhose is she talking about? As we filed off to the science block, Hawkeye was in a super-duper strop for some reason. She made me remove my armband and she was marching up and down looking at people like a Doberman, only much taller. And not a dog. She alarmed a first former so much that the first former fell into a holly bush and had to be fished out and sent to the nurse to calm down.

I said to Rosie, "I think widowhood has toughened me up. If Hawkeye gets on my case I am going to say to her, 'Hawkeye, sir, when you have suffered the torments of love like I have, you will not give a flying pig's bum about your Latin homework. Romulus and Remus could have been brought up by ostriches for all I care.'"

Rosie said, "Yeah right, well, let's see what happens when she gives you double detention."

"Do you know what I saw on TV the other night? Ostriches fall in love with human beings. On ostrich farms they go all gooey and even more dim when humans come to feed them. They try to snog them."

"Ostriches try to snog humans?"

"Yes."

"*Non.*"

"*Mais oui, mon petit idiot, c'est vrai.* It is very very *vrai.*"

"How can they snog when they have beaks?"

"You are being a bit beakist, Rosie."

Lunchtime

The Ace Gang are going on and on about the teenage werewolf party. Jas said, "Tom and I are going to wear matching false ears!" And then she had an uncontrollable laughing spaz.

I said, "Jas, when was the last time you saw a teenage werewolf with false ears?"

That made her stop snorting like a fool. She was all shuffily on the knicker toaster (radiator). "Well... it's, well... I mean..."

Rosie – who is in an alarmingly good mood now that Sven is winging his way home on his sleigh – slapped me on the back and said, "What do you get when you cross a mouse with an elephant?"

We all just looked at her and she put her glasses on sideways and said, "Massive holes in the skirting board!"

I feel like a bean in a bikini, tossed around on the sea of life. Set apart from my mates because of heartbreakosity. I love them but how childish they seem, chatting on about false eyebrows. I may never wear extra body hair ever again.

3:00 p.m.

We should be having Hawkeye for English but she is too busy torturing people, so Miss Wilson will be taking most of our lessons this term. She is a tremendous div, so English will be more or less a free period.

Oh, what larks! We are doing *Macbeth* as our set play. Although Miss Wilson says we are not allowed to say its name: we have to call it "The Scottish Play", because it's bad luck to say its name. As I said to Rosie and Jools, "Hurrah! A play about blokes in tights talking in Och Aye language for a thousand years."

We've all been dished out parts and, tragically, Jas is going to be Lady MacScottishplay. Rosie, Jools and Ellen are the three witches and I am some complete twit in tights called Macduff. Nauseating P. Green is my wife, Lady Macduff. She is thrilled and keeps mooning over at me.

I don't see how I am supposed to be a bloke, because they are – as we all know – a complete mystery.

4:15 p.m.

On the way home Jas was looking at her hand and going, "Out damn spot."

I said, "It's not the spot on your hand you have to worry about, Jas, it's the huge lurker lurking on your chin."

That shut her up and got her feeling about.

Actually, she hasn't got a lurker on her chin, but if she goes on fingering it long enough she will have.

Home (ha)
5:00 p.m.

Oh brilliant, Angus has gone into my wardrobe and found some of my knickers to attack. He was ambling out of my room with his head through one of the legs like some sort of Arab sheikh. I kicked at him but he dodged out of the way. He was purring really loudly; he loves it when you get rough with him. He is a good example of the benefits of rough love. I should really give him a good kicking every day.

Kitchen
5:30 p.m.

Oh yum yum and *quelle surprise*, we are having *les delicieuses* fish fingers and frozen peas for our tea! I am sure that I am developing rickets: my legs look distinctly bendy. Vati came in in a hilariously good mood. He kissed me on the head even though I tried to dodge him. I said, "Father, I need my own space and frankly you are in it."

He just laughed and said, "I've just seen Colin and he and Sandy are having a *Lord of the Rings* party and we're all invited."

Mutti said, "What a hoot."

I said with great meaningosity, "Vati, I will never – and I repeat, never – be wearing an elf's outfit in this lifetime, and for the sake of any sensitive people on the planet – that is, me – I beg you not to consider green tights."

He just smiled and said, "I know you are secretly very thrilled, Georgia."

He and Mutti laughed. And Libby joined in with a very alarming sort of laughing. Like a mad Santa Claus and pig combined. "Hohohogoggyhoggyhog."

I don't know what they teach her at nursery school, but it's not how to be normal.

Only 6:30 p.m.

I wonder what time it is in Kiwi-a-gogo land? They are twenty-four hours ahead of us and it's Monday here, so it must be Tuesday there.

6:35 p.m.

Does that mean that SG knows what I will be wearing for the teenage werewolf party before I do?

Not that I will be going.

Will I?

I will be the last to know as usual.

Oh Baby Jesus and your cohorts, please make something really great happen. Otherwise I am going to bed. But I will wait for half an hour because I trust in your ultimate goodnosity.

7:35 p.m.

It's not much to ask, is it? But oh no, Baby Jesus is just too busy to make anything interesting happen. Maybe he is holding the pensioner inferno against me.

In the loo

Sitting in the loo of life contemplating my navel.

My navel sticks out a bit. Is it supposed to do that? I hope it's not unravelling. That would be the final straw.

Vati keeps books in the loo. How disgusting is that?

Pooing and reading. What is he reading? It's called *Live and Let Die*. How true.

8:30 p.m.
No one has bothered to ring me. I wonder why Dave the Laugh hasn't phoned me? I could phone him, but that would mean he might think I am keen on him.

Which I am not.

8:45 p.m.
Vati's book is about James Bond, who is a sort of special-agent-type thing. Vati probably thinks he is like James Bond. Which he would be, if James Bond was a porky bloke with a badger attachment.

9:00 p.m.
I am in the prime of my womanhood, nunga-nungas poised and trembling (attractively). Lips puckered up and in peak condition for a snogging fest.

And I am in bed.

At nine p.m.

9:05 p.m.

Not alone for long, because my sister is now in bed with me. She has got her bedtime book for me to read to her. *Heidi.* About some girl who goes up a mountain in Swisscheeseland to live with some elderly mad bloke in lederhosen, who sadly for her is her grandfather.

I know how she feels. At least my grandad doesn't wear leather shorts. Yet.

9:15 p.m.

So far Heidi and Old Mr Mad of the Mountains have herded up goats and eaten a lot of cheese. A LOT. They are constantly eating cheese.

9:20 p.m.

Even Libby was so bored by the cheese extravaganza that she nodded off to sleep, so I slipped downstairs to phone Jas. I did it quietly because there will only be the usual tutting explosion from Vati about me using the phone if he hears me.

I whispered, "Jas?"

"Oh, it's you."

"What do you mean?"

"Well, I've got my jimmyjams on and I was reading my book about the wilderness course that Tom and I are going to go on."

"Oh I am sooooooo sorry, Jas, soooo sorry to interrupt your twig work just because I am all on my own without the comfort of human company and my life is ebbing away."

There was silence at the other end of the phone.

"Jas, are you still there?"

Her voice sounded a bit distant. "Yes."

I said, "What is that cracking noise?"

"Er..."

"You are actually playing with twigs, aren't you?"

"Well... I..."

How pathetico.

She said all swottily, "Look, I have to go. I've got my German homework to do."

"Don't bother learning their language, they are obsessed with goats."

"What are you talking about?"

"Lederhosen-a-gogo-land people are obsessed with goats... and cheese."

"Who says so?"

"It's in a book I am reading about them."

"What book?"

"It's called *Heidi*. It is utterly crap."

"*Heidi?*"

"*Jah.*"

Mrs Picky Knickers sounded all swotty and know-it-all. "*Heidi* is a children's book about a girl who lives in the Alps in Switzerland."

"Yes, and your point is?"

"That's not Germany."

"It's very near."

"You might as well say that Italy and France are the same because they are very near."

"I do say that."

"Or Italy and Greece."

"I say that as well."

"You talk rubbish."

"Yeah but I don't play with twigs like a... like a fringey thrush."

She slammed the phone down on me.

Well. She is so annoying.

But on the other hand, no one else is around to talk to.

Phoned her back.

"Jas, I'm sorry, you always hurt the one you love."

"Don't start the love thing."

"OK, but night-night."

"Night."

10:00 p.m.

Oh, I am so restless and bored. I think my mouth may be sealing over because of lack of snogging. Or shrinking. I wonder if that can happen? They say "Use It or Lose It" on all those really scary posters in the doctor's surgery, mainly for very very old people who are too lazy to walk about, and then their legs shrink, possibly. But it may be the same for lips.

10:05 p.m.

No sign of any shrinkage on the basooma front.

In the loo

11:00 p.m.

In Dad's James Bond book it says, "Bond came and stood close against her. He put a hand over each breast. But still she looked away from him out of the window. 'Not now,' she said in a low voice."

Now I am completely baffled. What in the name of arse does that mean?

A hand over each nunga?

Like a human nunga-nunga holder.

Do boys do that?

Wednesday March 9th

No letters from the Sex God.

And I haven't heard anything from Dave the Laugh either.

Still, what do I care, I am full of glaciosity for him.

I wonder if he will go to the party on Saturday. Not that I am interested, as I will be at home embroidering toilet roll holders or whatever very sad spinsters do.

Bathroom

7:30 a.m.

Oh fabulous, I have a lurking lurker on my cheek. The painters are due in this week and that is probably why I am feeling so moody.

That and the fact that my life is utterly crap.

Still, a really heavy period should cheer me up.

Maybe if I disguise the lurker with some eye pencil it will look like a beauty spot.

Breakfast

Mutti said, "Georgia, why don't you just hang a sign on your head that says, 'Have you noticed I've got a spot, everybody?'"

I tried to think of something clever to say to her but I am too tired.

8:20 a.m.

I was dragging myself out the door to another day of unnatural torture (school) when the postman arrived. It takes him about a year to get up our driveway because he tries to dodge Angus. Angus loves him. He is his little postie pal. The postie, who is not what you would call blessed in the looks department, was furtively looking around and shuffling about. I said helpfully, "Angus is off on his morning constitutional, so I am afraid you can't play with him."

The postie said, "I know what I would like to do with him and it involves a sack and a river. Here you are."

And he shoved a letter at me. Not ideal behaviour from a servant of the people I don't think.

Then I noticed it was an aerogram-type letter. For me. From Kiwi-a-gogo land. From the Sex God.

Oh joy joy joy joyitty joy joy.

And also thrice joy.

I looked at the writing. So Sex-Goddy. And it said "Georgia Nicolson" on it.

That was me.

And on the back it said:

From Robbie Jennings
R.D. 4
Pookaka lane (honestly)
Whakatane
New Zealand

That was him. The Sex God. I started skipping down the street until unfortunately I saw Mark Big Gob and his lardy mates. He doesn't even bother to look at my face, he just talks to my nungas.

Mark was leery like a leering thing and he said, "Careful,

Georgia, you don't want to knock yourself out with your jugs." And they all laughed.

Thank goodness I had worn my special sports nunga holder, or my "over-the-shoulder-boulder-holder", as Rosie calls it. At least my basoomas were nicely encased. Anyway, ha di hahahaha to Mark Big Gob – nothing could upset me today because I was filled with the joyosity of young love.

I did stop skipping though, and walked off with a dignity-at-all-times sort of walk.

But Mark still hadn't had his day; he shouted after me, "I'll carry them to school for you if you like!"

He is disgusting. And a midget lover. I don't know how I could have ever snogged him.

8:35 a.m.

Jas was stamping around outside her house going, "Oh *brrrrr*, it is so nippy noodles, *brr*!"

She had a sort of furry bonnet over her beret. I said, "You look like a crap teddy bear."

She just went on shivering and said, "Do you think we will get let off hockey because of Antarctic conditions?"

"Jas, you live, as I have always said, in the land of the

terminally deluded and criminally insane. Nothing gets us off hockey. We are at the mercy of a Storm Trooper and part-time lesbian. Miss Stamp LOVES Antarctic conditions. You can see her moustache bristling with delight when it snows."

If Jas has to wear a furry bonnet in cold weather, I don't think much of her chances of survival on her survival-type course.

Still, that is life.

Or in her case, death.

She was still going *"Brrr brr,"* but I didn't let it spoil my peachy mood.

"Jas, guess what? Something *très très magnifique* has happened at last."

"Brrr."

"Shut up *brrring*, Jas."

I got out my aerogram.

"Look, it's from SG."

"What does it say?"

"I don't know."

"Why not?"

"Because I haven't opened it yet, I am savouring it."

"It's not a pie."

"I know that, Jas. Please don't annoy me. I don't want to have to beat you within an inch of your life so early in the day."

I tucked the aerogram down the front of my shirt for safe keepies as we trudged up the hill to Stalag 14. But I had a song in my heart.

"Jas, I have a song in my heart, and do you know what it is?"

But she just ran off into the cloakroom to sit on the knicker toaster for a few minutes to thaw out.

Still, I did have a song in my heart called "I Have a Letter from a Sex God in my Over-the-shoulder-boulder-holder".

Assembly

Slim told us exciting news this morning. Elvis Attwood, the most bonkers man in Christendom and part-time caretaker, is retiring. We started cheering but had to change our cheering into a sort of "For He's a Jolly Good Fellow" thing because Hawkeye was giving us her ferret eye. Slim was rambling on in her jelloid way, chins shaking like billyo.

"So, as a special thank you for all the magnificent work Mr Attwood has put in over the years, we will be having a going-away party for him. We will have music and so on, and perhaps Mr Attwood will show us how to 'get with it', as you girls say."

She laughed like a ninny. Get with it? What in the name of her enormous undergarments is she raving on about? The last time Elvis did any dancing he had to be taken to the casualty department. So every cloud has a silver lining.

I said to the Ace Gang as we trailed out of Assembly to RE, "What started out as a scheissenhausen day has turned out to be a groovy gravy day."

I am looking forward to RE because while everyone has their little snooze I can read my letter from the beloved.

RE

We all snuggled down at the back. RoRo was knitting something for the teenage werewolf party. I think it might be a full-length beard. Jools was doing her cuticles and Jas was reading her wilderness manual. She loves it because it has lots of photos of girlie swots building incomprehensible things out of twigs. Anyway, time to read my letter. Miss Wilson was beginning to ramble on about "world peace" and asking us for our views. I didn't want to have to answer anything, I just wanted her to soothingly write stuff on the board or rave on. So I put my hand up. That startled her. I said, "Miss Wilson, I have been very troubled in my mind."

That started Rosie off in uncontrollable sniggering. Miss Wilson looked at me through her owly glasses. She is the most strangely put together person I have ever come across. Where does she get her clothes from? Did you know that you could get dresses made out of red felt with matching booties for grown-ups? She has clearly been to the circus shop that Slim buys her wrinkly elephant-tights from.

Anyway, Miss Wilson was vair vair interested in my troubled mind.

"Is it something of a theological nature, Georgia?"

"Yes indeedy, Miss Wilson. This is what is troubling me. If God is, you know, impotent..."

Miss Wilson went sensationally red, so now her head matched her booties.

"Well... er... Georgia, erm, *impotent* means not being able to have any children... I rather think you mean *omnipotent*."

"Whatever. Well, if He is, does that mean that He is with you even when you are in the lavatory?"

Miss Wilson started rambling on about God not being really a bloke like other geezers but more of a spiritual whatsit. Hmmm. She has a very soothing manner. Jools had finished her cuticles and was having a little zizz on her pencil case.

I opened my letter with trembly hands. I wondered how long it would take me to fly to Kiwi-a-gogo land.

Dear Georgia,

Sorry it has taken me so long to write to you but it has been full-on since I got here. The countryside around here is fantastic, it's all formed from volcanic activity. There are volcanoes near here that are still live and there is a lot of geothermal activity.

Yesterday when we were eating our lunch outside, the table was heaving and lurching about. That's because the molten steam trapped beneath the Earth's crust makes the ground move and shake around. It was amazing! The sheep were going backwards and forwards, and the trees were going up and down. There *are bore fields around the whole area where they tap the steam and make electricity out of it. The lads took me to see a rogue bore called Old Faithful that explodes every fifteen minutes.*

Rogue bore? He could have stayed here and just sat still in our school for a few minutes; it's full of rogue bores. Sadly, they do not explode.

And that is all the letter was about, just loads and loads of stuff about vegetables and sheep and lurching tables. Not one thing about missing me.

I couldn't believe it.

At the end, it said,

Well, I must go, some of the guys are going down to the river. It has natural hot springs that run through it. We go down there at night and lie in it playing our guitars.

He was going down to a river and he was going to lie in it. That was the big nightspot.

I wrote a note to Jas.

♡ 53

Jas,

SG just talked about opossums and rogue bores and a river and then at the end he said, "I hope you are well and happy. You're a great girl. Gidday. Robbie x"

One measly kiss.

11:00 a.m.

After RE I was in a state of shock. I could hardly eat my cheesy snacks. We sat on the knicker toaster in the Blodge lab and the Ace Gang had a look at the letter.

Jas said, "Well, he said you were a great girl."

I just looked at her.

"And it's really interesting about the molten steam and the geothermal... stuff."

I just looked at her again.

Rosie said, "Forget him, he's obsessed with marsupials. When he comes back he'll be playing a didgeridoo and be like Rolf Harris. Move on."

4:15 p.m.

Walking home with Jas. I said to her, "I cannot believe my

life. I've kept reading SG's letter over and over but it still rambles on about steam and vegetables."

Jas looked thoughtful (crikey) and then she said something almost bordering on the very nearly not mad. She said, "Maybe it's in code."

"In code?"

"Yes, so that, erm, the customs people, or say it fell into the wrong hands, like your mum and dad... well, so that they couldn't tell what he had really written."

I gave her a hug. "Jas, I am sorry that I ever doubted your sanity. You are a genius of the first water."

In my room
4:45 p.m.
So let's see.

5:30 p.m.
If I underline every fourth word, that might work.

6:00 p.m.
I think I have got it! Phoned Jas.

"Jas, I think I've got it."

"Go on then."

"OK. It's sort of in shorthand even when it is decoded but... anyway... this is what it says:

'Dear Georgia. Me, you fantastic. When we were heaving and lurching about it was amazing. Me explodes every fifteen minutes. At night me in it playing you. You're great. Love Robbie.'"

There was a silence. Then Jas said, "Did you say, 'me explodes every fifteen minutes'?"

"Yes... keen, isn't he?"

In bed
7:00 p.m.

It wasn't in code. It was just a really, really crap letter.

Nothing can be worse than how I feel now.

7:30 p.m.

Wrong. I cannot believe my vati. He has sold our normal(ish) car and bought a Robin Reliant. You know, one of those really really sad cars that only the very mad buy? It has got three wheels. It is a three-wheeled car. I shouted down to Vati, "Why?"

He was all preened-up and dadish.

He shouted back up, "It's an antique."

I tried logic with him. "Vati, sometimes antiques are interesting – the crown jewels, for instance, they interest me – but this is just a really old crap car that only has three wheels."

He was polishing it. It's red and it has a racing strip.

Vati said, "Hop in and I'll take you for a spin."

As if.

Dad started rustling around in the boot and shouted to Mum, "Connie, come on, I'll take you and Libby for a ride in the Sexmobile."

He is so ludicrously pleased with himself.

And Mutti was as bad. All dillydollyish and also she had a tiny skirt on. At least she had on a skirt though, unlike Libby, who was in the nuddy-pants.

8:00 p.m.

In the end they all went off, including Angus, who I actually thought was driving the car at first. He had his paws on the steering wheel and was looking straight ahead. Even though I am on the rack of love, it did make me laugh. Then Vati's head popped up. Not content with the humiliatorosity of the Robin Reliant clown car, Vati also bought a Second World War flying helmet and goggles.

As they drove off, he wound down the window and shouted, "Chocks away!!!"

What does Mutti see in him? He must have been like this when she met him. Which means, in essence, that she likes porky blokes with badgers on their chins who are clearly mental.

At this rate I am going to spend the rest of my life with them, so I should get used to it, I suppose.

8:05 p.m.
I can't. I would rather plunge my head into a basket of whelks.

8:10 p.m.
What is it with boys?

I may do some research on them for my part in *MacUseless* or *The Och Aye Play*.

I may as well, as my so-called mates can't be bothered to ring me.

8:30 p.m.

Phone rang.

If it's Dave the Laugh, I am going to give him the full force of my glaciosity. I hate boys.

It was Rosie.

"Gee?"

"Oh hi, I'm glad you rang because I am sooo—"

"Did you hear about the dog who went into a pub and said to the barman, 'Can I have a pint and a bag of crisps please?'"

"Rosie, I don't—"

"The barman said, 'Blimey, that's brilliant. There's a circus in town. You should go and get a job.'"

"Rosie, I have—"

"And the dog said, 'Why? Do they need electricians?'"

And she slammed down the phone.

I am seriously worried about her dwindling sanity. I'd just got back upstairs to my bed of pain when the phone rang again. Why can't we have a portable fandango thing or, alternatively, a servant called Juan who answers it?

Is it so much to ask?

This time it was Ellen.

"Georgia, it's me. I was, you know... for the party. Well, do

♥ 59

you... think I... well, if you were me, would you or would you just kind of, you know... or not?"

What in the name of Hitler's pants and matching bra set is she on about?

"Ellen, how can I put this? What in the name of arse are you talking about?"

"Dave the Laugh, should I, you know, well, would you?"

Oh marvellous, I have to be Wise Woman of the Forest for my mates. Also it reminded me that if Ellen found out about the Dave the Laugh snogging scenarios, there might well be fisticuffs at dawn.

Still, I am not God and also I am very very busy with my own problems. My lurking lurker has to be dealt with before it makes a surprise appearance. Not that I will ever be going out again anyway. My lurker could grow to the size of my head if it wanted to. Erlack, now I feel sick.

Ellen was rambling on and on about Dave the Laugh and how to entice him and so on. In the end, in sheer desperadoes, I said, "Look, do you know why Dave the Laugh is called, you know, Dave the Laugh?"

Ellen said, "Er. No, why is that?"

I am being pushed to the limits of my nicosity, but I tried, God knows I tried.

"He's called that because he likes a laugh, and well, to be frank, Ellen, you are a bit lacking *vis-à-vis* the laughometer scale."

9:00 p.m.

I wish when I am speaking complete and utter bollocks people would not take me seriously. It's not my fault that I have advised Ellen to develop an infectious laugh, is it? Oh, I am so tired.

9:30 p.m.

By the time the Circus Family came home, I was tucked up in my bed with the lights off. Not that it makes any difference whatsoever.

Sure enough, it was tramp, tramp up the stairs. Open door, blinding light as Mutti switched it on. Swiss Family Mad came and sat on my bed. Angus now had the goggles on and a scarf round his neck.

Mutti said, "Oh, it was really good fun, Georgie."

Libby got in bed with me and started prodding my lurker, going, "Spottie bottie boy."

♡ 61

Then Vati came in. Into my bedroom. He was looking at me and I was only wearing my pyjamas.

I said, "Did anyone notice that my light was off and that I was asleep? Did anyone get that?"

But they just went on chattering and giggling, and Vati was playing tickly bears with Libby and Mutti.

Please save me.

Thursday March 10th
Maths

I am going to have to kill Rosie – she is soo overexcited about the return of Sven. Every time Miss Stamp turns round she does mad disco dancing. Miss Stamp turned round a bit sharpish and caught Rosie nodding her head like a loon. She said, "Rosemary Mees, what are you doing?"

Rosie said, "I was agreeing with your excellent point on the roundness of circles."

She got a bad conduct mark for cheek, but she is still as mad as a hen.

She sent me a note: What swings round and round a cathedral wrapped in cellophane?

I tried to ignore her but she kept looking and raising her

eyebrows until I thought she would have a nervy spaz. So I mouthed back, "What?" and she sent another note: The lunchpack of Notre Dame.

Dear God, am I never to be free?

English

Oh rave on, rave on. Not content with boring us to death with *MacUseless*, we are also doing two more books. *Wuthering Heights*, or *Blithering Heights*, as we call it, and *Samuel Pepys' Diary*, about this horrifically boring bloke called Samuel Pepys. He quite literally, from what I can gather, peeps about. He just looks up ladies' skirts most of the time and says "prithee". Still, we all have to accept he is a genius. On the plus side, the dirty bits will make Miss Wilson go completely spazoid.

4:30 p.m.

Walking home with Jas and Rosie when we saw Dave the Laugh and Rollo and Tom. Jas went ludicrously girlish, even though she has been seeing Hunky for about a zillion years. I should know – I am like that bloke, Pepys's mate... Boswell, who had to write down all the boring stuff that Pepys did because he was his secretary or something.

I could write a diary about Jas: "Prithee it bee Thursdayee and Missee Jas gotte uppee this morning and puttee on her pantee forsooth and lack a day, her bottom I declareth groweth by the minutee."

I had a bit of a nervy spaz when I saw Dave. He was all cool. Rats. He said, "Easy girls, don't be selfish, there's more than enough of me to go round."

I gave him my glacial look but he just winked at me. I couldn't smile even if I wanted to because I had got so much lurker eradicator (cover-up) on that I couldn't move my face.

Rosie said, "Are you coming to Sven's teenage werewolf party on Saturday? There will be snacks."

Rollo said, "It's not fish fingers, is it?"

Rosie looked pityingly at him. "Rollo, keep up, this is a teenage werewolf party."

Dave the Laugh said, "Babies' tiny heads then, is it?"

Rosie said, "Now you are ignoring the sophisticosity of the occasion. It is of course sausages with lashings of tomato ketchup."

Dave said, "Of course it is. See you later, chicklets. And

Georgia, it is useless trying to ignore me – it just gives me the Mega Horn."

And he and the lads went off whistling the theme from *The Italian Job*.

4:45 p.m.
How annoying is that?

I could kill him.

He completely ignored my glaciosity.

Rosie and Jas were looking at me in a looking-at-me sort of way. Which I hate. Tom walked along with us. Jas was wittering on to him and holding his hand.

"I've found this stuff in the library about different kinds of fungi you can eat. You know, for our wilderness thing. Well, if we got lost away from the others in the group we could eat it and not starve."

I said, "Forgive me if I'm right, but are you talking about mushrooms?"

Jas got all huffy. "Well. All YOU are interested in is Dave the Laugh."

I tried to look as bewildered as a bee who finds itself in an egg-cup hat.

"I am not at all interested in Dave the Stupid Laugh – it's just that I am even less interested in grey shapeless things that lurk about the woods."

They were all looking at me still.

I tried again. "Oh come on, get real... Dave the Laugh, I – me – I mean..."

Tom said, "So you do like him then?"

Jas said meaningfully, "Yes, well, SOME people know SOMETHING about SOMETHING."

Oh good point, well made. Not.

I wanted to kill her and make her eat her fringe. And her knickers.

Rosie, who had been practising being blind and using me as her guide dog, said, "I've got an uncle in Yorkshire who eats cow udder as a treat."

That can't be true.

Can it?

5:00 p.m.

Walking home all alone.

I let myself in when I got to our house.

I opened the door and yelled out, "Hello Georgia darling,

take your coat off and come and warm yourself by this blazing fire! I've made a nourishing stew for you, and when your father comes home from being really masculine and rich we can talk about the four hundred pounds a week you need for a decent pad in London."

As if.

6:00 p.m.
Mum is out tossing herself around a room full of red-faced loons in leotards. Again. Who knows where Dad is. Out in his clown car causing havoc.

Brrr, it is so nippy noodles and dark.

Got into bed it was so chilly bananas.

Oh I am so cold and bored.

7:00 p.m.
Phone rang. It was Ellen.

"I heard you saw Dave on the way home and he's definitely coming on Saturday because he said he was and that means he is. Do you think?"

I said, "Put it this way, there will be snacks and Sven possibly in a Viking outfit, of course Dave the Laugh will be there."

And then Ellen started doing this thing. I thought she was having a fit at first. She was snorting and going "Hnnurknurkhhhhnuuuuuurkkk."

"Ellen, what are you doing?"

"I'm practising my infectious laugh."

Good grief.

Bedroom

I am so depressed and bored I may even have to do some homework.

In Mutti's bedroom

7:15 p.m.

I wonder if Mutti has got anything new I could wear to the party.

Ho hum.

I have squirted my lurker with her Opium. I think it might be retreating to where it came from. Although with my luck it will probably re-emerge on the end of my nose, giving me that two-nosed look that is so popular amongst the very very ugly.

7:30 p.m.

I haven't even got the heart to write to the Sex God, otherwise known as Marsupial Man. He'll probably be lying in a river somewhere anyway.

7:40 p.m.

My new address is:

  Georgia Nicolson

  Crap House

  Crapton-on-sea

  Crapshire

  Crapland

7:45 p.m.

What is this book that Mutti has hidden in her knicker drawer?

  How to Make Anyone Fall in Love with You.

8:00 p.m.

This is amazing.

8:30 p.m.

Phoned Rosie.

"Rosie."

"*Quoi?*"

"Do you know how to make anyone fall in love with you?"

"Well, in Sven's case I reel him in with snacks and snogging."

I've seen the two of them snogging and eating snacks at the same time, so I didn't really want to talk about it much.

I went on, "My mutti's got a secret book and it tells you how to make anyone fall in love with you, even normal boys, boys who are not Svens."

Friday March 11th

Odds bodkin, what is the matter with grown-ups? They are all mad as hens (madder). Usually when you do plays you just read them out in order and so on. Not at this hellhole. Miss Wilson decided we had to "get into" our parts by improvising. How crap is that? Very, very very and thrice very crap.

Off we all lolloped to the gym, where we had to "be" different colours to music. Rosie, who as we know is not entirely normal at the best of times, almost hung herself with one of the gym ropes when she was being purple.

All of the Ace Gang (apart from Swotty Knickers) got a bad conduct mark when Miss Wilson spotted that we were doing "Let's go down the disco" dance to every colour.

Nauseating P. Green is loving it, though. Tottering and blundering around. When we had to be "very very tiny", she crept round barging into benches and gym mats. Sadly, then we had to do "very big", and it was only quick thinking by Ellen that prevented P. Green from destroying the cassette player with her elephantine feet. If the safety inspector had popped in, the school would have been closed down.

But then the next worst thing happened – Mr Attwood came bonkering around. He came into the gym with his flat cap on and his ridiculous overalls that he only wears to keep his fags in. We were being items of food (I was being an egg and Rosie was being a sausage). Anyway, Elvis said, "This area is for the use of physical education as stated on the schedule."

Miss Wilson tried to explain, "We're improvising Shakespeare, Mr Attwood."

Mr Attwood was not impressed. He said, "That's as may be, Miss, but it's not on the timetable and the gym mats are in a state of disarray."

He went off harrumphing about, complaining and muttering and holding his back as he moved around.

Oh, how we will miss his jolly cheerful ways when he leaves. Not.

Still, he had got us out of being bits of food.

I patted him on the back as I went by.

He went sensationally ballistic, even for him.

"I've seen you, prancing around like a fool. I know what you're up to. I've locked my hut."

Quite, quite scarily mad. As we loped slowly back to the classroom, I said to Jas, "Mr Attwood is being unusually insane, isn't he? He will be going to the insane caretakers' home when he retires. Do you think he's got senile dyslexia like my grandad?"

Jas was a bit flustered and red because, sadly, she had enjoyed the workshop. Her hair was all stuck up on end. She said, "You mean senile dementia."

"Whatever, Jas, you are getting very picky, which is a shame because your fringe is all sticky-uppy."

She dashed off to the loos to wet it down, just in case she sees Hunky on the way home. She is very vain.

6:00 p.m.

I have decided that life has to go on and I have an obligation to the Ace Gang to force myself to go to the teenage werewolf party.

6:30 p.m.

Also I want to show Dave the Laugh that I am not remotely interested in him.

8:00 p.m.

What is it with parents?

Usually they don't take any notice of you, always saying "Be quiet!" or "Go to your room!", etc. But when you want to be quiet and go to your room with your mates, they won't leave you alone.

Ellen, Jools, Rosie, Mabs, Jas and me were trying out different make-up techniques and hairstyles and then it was *tap tap tap* on the door – a door which, by the way, had a clear notice attached to it that said, politely, "Go away, everyone, and that means you Mutti and Vati in particular, but also Libby and Angus." I know Libby and Angus can't read yet, so I had pinned a photo of Libby, looking particularly attractive in the nuddy-pants but wearing a pan on her head, and I had put a line through it, and for Angus I just did a big paw mark with a cross through it.

Vati barged in and we all started screaming.

He said, "Hi, girlies, do you want a little spin in my new car?"

I said to him, "Vati: a) you are banned from my room and b) do I look like the sort of person who is stupid and mad?"

Unfortunately we were all having egg masks at the time, so we did look like the stupid and mad.

8:30 p.m.

I put the chest of drawers against the door so that no one could get in.

I said, "I am going for the sophisticated werewolf look: black, black and just a hint of black, with black lipstick."

Ellen said, "Is there anyone going to the party that you fancy?"

Jas looked at me – she had her fringe in a roller, which made her look even more ridiculisimus than normal, but that didn't stop her from doing her looking thing.

I looked back with my very worst look. But it didn't stop her.

She went on and on in between mouthfuls of cheesy Wotsits. "Yes, Georgia, is there going to be anyone at the party that you might have a LAUGH with?"

I hate her. I hate her.

I said, "Well, you never know, do you? I have to try and have a life after SG. I've made a little shrine to him. Do you want to see it?"

I'd hidden the shrine under a cloth so that it was a very secret thing. Unfortunately, when I took the cloth off, Jesus had come unstuck and crashed over into Buddha, and they looked like they were snogging. The photo of Robbie is the one he gave me when I went round to his house for the first snogging extravaganza. It's one of him lying on his bed just looking into the camera. God, he's so gorgey and when he looks into the camera it's like he is looking right into my heart. I could feel tears welling up in my eyes.

The Ace Gang were really nice to me. Rosie put her arm round me and said, "Just think of him surrounded by marsupials."

To change the subject in case I did uncontrollable weeping I showed them Mutti's book, which I have sneaked into my room.

They all sat down on my bed and I started to read stuff out. They were ogling me like goosegogs.

I said, "OK, this is really cool, it tells you how to become a boy magnet *extraordinaire*. There's a list. Number one is, let me see, oh yes... 'Smile broadly'."

We practised smiling broadly. Good grief, how scary Jas is when she smiles broadly. Surely boys don't like this? Perhaps I read it wrong. Nope, it definitely says that boys like you to smile broadly. Still, there are limits.

I said to Jas, "Jas, if you don't mind me saying, your broad smile is a bit scary potatoes."

She went all huffy and red.

"Well, you've got some room to talk, Georgia. When you smile broadly your nose is about four feet wide."

Oh charming. That is the thanks you get for trying to be a good pal.

Ellen said, "OK, my face is aching a bit from the smiling thing. What's the next tip?"

I looked at the book. "'Throw him darting glances.'"

We practised throwing each other darting glances. Easy peasy.

Number three was "Dance alone to the music." I put on

a CD and we practise

my new taut and all-er

really do keep my nung

wildly in the air and jigg

music.

I shouted to Jas above the

of nip nip emergence in this top

She began peering at my nung

"Stop it, lezzie, I only asked you

emergence. I didn't ask you to ogle my nungas.

She really got the megahump then and tried *ignorez-vous*ing me. She didn't storm off in a strop though, because she wanted to know what number four on the list was. I said, "Okey-dokey, number four is... 'Look straight at him and flip your hair.'"

We did excellent hair flipping. Which is what we mostly do all day anyway.

Number five was "Look at him, look away, toss your head and then look back." There was a lot of tossing and so on until I got a really bad neck cramp.

Number six was quite hilarious. "Lick your lips and parade close to him with exaggerated hip movements."

round the room. I said, "Surely boys
ook like you've got replacement hips."
was a bit more sensible. It said you had to
. You have to sort of look him in the eyes and
our eyes away from his as if they've been stuck
m toffee.
my house it is quite likely that you could wake up with
fee in your eyes, but I don't suppose that's what the
author had in mind.

10:00 p.m.
The girls all crashed off home with plenty of things to think
about and practise for tomorrow. I watched them out my
window doing the hip thing down the street, like elderly
hula dancers in overcoats.

I felt a bit cheered up.

Midnight
Only nineteen hours till the party.

12:05 a.m.
What do I care though? I have given up boys.

12:13 a.m.

How weird is this? There is a bit in the book about different cultural ways of entrancing boys. It says that in Mongolia when the woman is in the mood (i.e. full of red-bottomosity) she puts out a flag. Then when the man comes by, he sees the flag and races off to get his lasso and horse. Then she runs off and he chases her on his horse and lassos her.

12:20 a.m.

Night-night one and all.

Saturday March 12th

11:00 a.m.

Woken up at dawn, even though I should be getting lots of beauty sleep. Mutti was yelling and going ballisticisimus. She was shouting, "You horrible horrible brute!"

Well, she only has herself to blame, it was her who married him.

I hauled myself up to see what fresh hell was going on. At the kitchen door Mutti was hurling things at Angus, who was sitting in the flowerbed with a bat's ear in his mouth just out of her range.

Mutti was very very red and wearing her dressing gown, which isn't very nice for community relations, as it is practically transparent. She was going on and on. "This so-called bloody pet of yours is... is... It's like a graveyard for small rodents in our house. I wouldn't mind but he gets through about a ton of cat food a day. Big BRUTE!!!"

Shouting at Angus, in my humble opinion, is as useless as challenging a centipede to an arse-kicking contest. But I didn't say. Instead I tried the reasoned sensible approach for which I am famous.

"Mutti, you see the thing is, you are hurting Angus's feelings by yelling at him. I think he's crying."

"He will be crying when I get hold of him. If he lives long enough to cry."

She is so violent. I said, "In my cat book it explains things; you see, Angus brings you birds and bats' ears and stuff because he thinks you are a really useless cat in the nuddy-pants. He thinks you are too dim and stupid to catch your own snacks. The bat ear is his little gift to you. And you are yelling at him. He is very puzzled and upset."

By this stage Angus was lying on his back with the bat ear caught between his front paws, tossing it about. Not crying as such.

12:30 p.m.

Back in my bedroom to start preparations.

I've done the base coat of my nails, toes and fingers. Now then, what is next on my list in order? Ah yes, relax your mind.

I lay down on my bed with a cucumber slice over each eye. Ahhhhh. Let go of all tension.

Fat chance. Libby came barging in singing, "Sex bum, sex BUM, I'm a sex bum!" Which I think is unsuitable for a four year old.

I managed to get Libby out of my room and put her into the airing cupboard – she likes it up there. Vati was in the drive cleaning his clown car. I have asked him if he will wear a mask when he goes out in it. Actually I have asked him to wear a mask at all times, but you might as well ask for the moon. I opened my bedroom window and yelled down at him.

"Vati, my dear little sister doesn't sing 'Bar bar bag sheet' any more, nor does she sing 'Three blind lice'. Do you know what she does sing?"

He was too busy polishing the clown car to take any notice. In fact, if I had gone to Kiwi-a-gogo land and a very fat Eskimo called Carl had moved into my bedroom, he still wouldn't have noticed. I don't know why people bother having children if they are going to spend the whole time pretending they don't exist. I went on regardless, like Sherpa Tensing.

"As you ask, I will tell you what she sings. She sings 'Sex bum, sex bum, I'm a sex bum.'"

And he laughed.

I said, "I hope you find it as amusing when she turns out to be a child prostitute."

By the time I looked round from the window, Libby was back in my bed with her *Heidi* book.

"Heggo, Gingey, time to read."

I tried to explain to her that I am busy and have to get ready to go out, but she gave me a glancing blow with scuba-diving Barbie.

I have at least managed to keep Angus out of my room. I have closed the door. Libby thinks it's very funny because Angus knows we are in here and he keeps putting his paw under the door and groping around.

But he can stay out there. I don't want bat essence on my party things.

4:00 p.m.

No wonder small children are mad. Heidi, who is still living with her mad grandad in the mountains, is clearly a bit on the insane side from the beginning, because it says, "It was with a happy heart that Heidi lay down on her bed of hay."

Good Lord.

4:30 p.m.

Then this boy called Peter is jealous of Heidi's new friend (some soppy nitwit in a wheelchair). So he pushes the soppy nitwit's wheelchair off the edge of the mountain while the soppy nitwit is having some cheese in the house.

(I must make a note to myself to NEVER go to Swisscheese-a-gogo land.)

5:00 p.m.

Ah well, it all ends happily as the soppy nitwit learns to walk because she hasn't got a wheelchair any more.

So, in conclusion, this is the moral of *Heidi*: always push invalid chairs off the top of mountains when you get the opportunity. The end.

Excellent advice.

7:00 p.m.

Time to go. I think I look rather groovy and mysterious in my teenage werewolf outfit. I decided against the black lipstick in the end because it made me look a bit like those sad Goths who turn up at gigs in the summer in leather bondage stuff and then have to sit really still because they are too hot to live. And then they stick to the seats.

Also, I have some new and groovy lippy and lip gloss in different flavours.

Très très gorgey and *bon*.

Went downstairs for Vati's traditional lecture about the length of my skirt, make-up, curfew time, drinking, snogging or anything. I hate it when he talks to me like a so-called grown-up. It's very embarrassing in a clown car owner. He was slumped on the sofa as normal. Gosh, he is porkus bigus these days. I said, "Vati, I really think that you should get in shape."

He didn't even look round. He just said, "I am in shape. Round is a shape."

While he was laughing like a loon at his *très pathétique* joke I slipped quietly out the front door.

Escape!! Freedom!!! Party!!!!

Not that I am really cheered up.

Just brave.

7:45 p.m.

We all met up at the clock tower and walked to Rosie's together.

As we went through the gate I said to Jas, "Rosie's mutti and vati are always away; how sensible and reasonable they are. All my mutti and vati do is hang around the house asking me what I am doing and also why am I doing it and when am I going to stop doing it."

Jas, representative for the terminally annoying, said, "My olds have given me my own key... It's a sort of token of my passage into adulthood."

I said, "Are you sure it's the key to your house? Perhaps it's the key to someone else's house and is therefore not a token of adulthood, but just their way of saying goodbye."

Hunky laughed and Jas gave him a "look", but as I was giggling at my own deep amusingosity she shoved me really hard and I nearly fell off my heels. My shoes, in keeping with my new sophisticosity, are quite high. In fact they are so high I may even be able to look Sven in the eye, which will be scary.

I am a bit nervous about seeing Dave the Laugh.

8:15 p.m.

Tom rang the bell and the door was ripped open by Sven. Yeah!! Sven back again. Crikey, I had forgotten how alarming he can be. Even by his (high) standards he had gone a lot too far this time. He had a Viking helmet on over an Afro wig and he was drinking out of a horn. He picked me and Jas up and said, "Hey swingers!! Coming on in why dontcha, chicks and laddies."

What planet does he live on? And how do you not go there?

Nice to see him, though. I have never seen furry shorts before.

Then Rosie popped up – she was entirely covered in fur: eyebrows and sidies, furry hands and knees, and even fur poking out of her shoes.

I said to her, "There is the suggestion of the wildebeest about Sven in those shorts."

And she said, "I know, exciting isn't it? Help yourself to snacks and drinks."

The pink chipolatas in tomato sauce really did look like severed fingers. Yum yum.

9:00 p.m.
Quite a crowd at the party. All the usual suspects: Sam and his mates from sixth-form college, the Foxwood crowd, Damion Knightly (known as the Dame) and his mates from St John's, plus loads of girls we knew from gigs and Moorgrange School. Some of the boys were quite fit, but none had that *je ne sais quoi*, that Sex Goddy charm that brought out the red-bottomosity in me.

And no sign of Dave the Laugh.

Good.

At least I could relax.

Jas said, "Dave the Laugh's not here."

I said, "So?"

And she just looked at me.

She is turning quite literally into a staring person.

9:15 p.m.
I thought just for a laugh I would try out some of the tactics from Mutti's book.

The Dame came over and said, "Hi, Gee, come and dance about like a prat."

And he pulled me on to the dance floor (the bit in between the sofa and the dining table). The Dame was blundering around to some really loud rock music that Sven had put on. Sven was actually on the table thrusting his furry shorts around like a sort of Viking lap dancer. Rosie was doing the twist very very fast till she was a blur of fur.

Anyway, I thought for practice I would try "sticky eyes" on the Dame. So I looked him in the eyes. He looked a bit startled at first, like he was thinking, "Oy what are you looking at, mate?" But I did that dragging my eyes away from his thing and then looking back. And it worked!!! He was sort of mesmerised. In fact it was a bit like I had hypnotised him. I kept looking him in the eye and then I moved to the fireplace, still looking at him. And he followed me there like a boy zombie. I went behind the TV and he followed me there. I went and stood by the window and he followed me there. It was amazing.

Then Dave the Laugh walked in. Gadzooks and also crikey!

He was dressed all in black like me and he looked cool.

His hair was slicked back and he had false fangs. Which I am alarmed to say I found a bit attractive. You could do excellent lip nibbling with them.

I had stopped looking at the Dame but he still followed me as I went to the snacks and drinks table. I was sort of casually pretending that I hadn't even noticed Dave the Laugh. Which was a bit difficult to keep up, because he shouted, "OK all you chicks who find me irresistible, follow me. No pushing."

Oh vair vair *amusant*. He's so bloody confident. He went off into the kitchen and a few girls (including Ellen, who as we know has no pride to speak of) went after him. I was just looking at the kitchen door when Dave suddenly appeared back through it again. I was so shocked that I turned round really quickly and practically snogged the Dame, who was lurking behind me.

He said, looking all dreamy and hypnotised, "Do you fancy going outside?"

I said, "Er, it's minus a million degrees out there."

And he said, "I'll keep you warm."

Is there a crap book that useless boys read called *Tips for Being Useless*? If there is, the Dame has read it. I didn't even bother replying. Then Ellen came dithering over to me. She was all red and spazzy.

"He's – you know, well, he's... I... should I... well, you know?"

I said, "Ellen, look, don't have a nervy b. It's not attractive. Listen, why don't you try that dancing-on-your-own tactic?"

She thought that was a good idea and started dancing around looking all dreamy and moody, and slightly swishing her hair about. Within seconds one of Sam's mates started dancing with her.

Surely this how-to-make-anyone-fall-in-love-with-you thing can't be this easy?

Dave the Laugh was looking at me, but I wasn't going for it, fangs or no fangs. I could go up to him and say, "Hi, Dave. Bye, Dave. You are so yesterday, but fangs for the memory."

Shut up, brain!!!!!

He was looking at me but he didn't come over, so I thought I would go look at the CD collection in a sort of cool way because the tension was making me want to go to the piddly-diddly department.

I had to walk past him to get to the CDs so I flicked my hair a bit and did the hip-waggling thing. (Which is not as easy to coordinate as you might think.)

Yess!!! Result is he followed me. I was looking at the CDs and didn't realise until the last minute that they were all upside down and I couldn't see the titles. He said, "Georgia."

I didn't even turn round.

"Georgia, I know your hips are bad but do you fancy a quick snog? I've got healing hands."

He is appalling!!!

It sort of made me laugh, though. He is soooo full of himself.

I turned round to him and looked at him like it said in the book (the bit I hadn't told the Ace Gang yet). It said, "Number eight. Let your eyes slide down the nose to the lips, caress the lips with your eyes for a moment and then slowly venture south to the neck."

Dave took his fangs out and said, "So, Sex Kitty..."

It was really weird because I felt like I was melting into Dave. And we would have snogged right there in front of everyone. I knew Ellen was there and I knew everyone would see and it would be dreadful, but all the blood in my brain had gone off on a little holiday to my lips.

Just then a girl's voice came into my head from behind Dave. It said, "Hi, Dave, sorry I'm late, I couldn't park my scooter."

Through the haze of frustrated snoggosity, I looked at the voice. It belonged to Rachel, a girl I know vaguely from hockey and gigs.

Rachel said, "Oh hi, Georgia, how's Stalag 14?"

I just went a bit goldfishy, opening my mouth but not saying anything. Dave looked like a rabbit caught in car headlights. Dave the rabbit eventually managed to speak. "Oh. Hi, Rachel," and he gave her a kiss on her cheeks.

She kissed him on the lips and put her arms round his neck. Then she pulled him away and said, "Come on, big boy, let's groove."

I just stood there.

Dave looked back at me and shrugged his shoulders. Then they went off into the other room. Rachel still had her arms around him.

I couldn't believe it.

It was unbelievable, that is why.

I couldn't stay.

I slipped out and got my coat and crept out into the dark night.

I waited until I got to the gate and into the street but then I just couldn't help it, tears started pouring out of my eyes.

Even though I would look like a panda in a skirt I didn't care.

I heard footsteps behind me. If it was Dave coming to apologise, he could just forget it. Then I heard Jas's voice. "Georgia, it's me, I'll – I'll walk back with you. I saw what happened."

She might be a complete and utter fringey annoyance, but Jas was my bestest pal.

She put her arm around me and said, "This is just friendly, it's not, you know... I'm not... er..."

I said, "Oh this is awful. It wasn't just that I was displaying glaciosity to Dave... it's well, I thought he wasn't just a snoggee but also a mate. He taught me the secrets of the Horn and now he's gone off with another girl..."

Jas went, "I know."

"Just went off immediately with another girl."

"I know."

"I'm not even warm in my grave."

"I know."

"She's got slightly ginger hair."

"I know."

"My smile is much nicer than hers."

"I know... er... hang on, is it?"

"Yes."

"Right."

"I am abandoned on the ship of life."

"I know."

"Jas, you are not really cheering me up."

"Well, I know, and that's because there is really nothing to be cheerful about; I would hate to be you."

In bed
11:45 p.m.

Jas says she will never sympathise with me again after I pulled her stupid hat down over her stupid face and she fell over a paving stone. That is the good news, but otherwise life is absolutely beyond the Valley of Crap and entering the Universe of Totally Useless.

Midnight

I lit a candle at my altar to Robbie (after I had removed scuba-diving Barbie and some chewed-up moth).

Why oh why did this happen to me? I must have done something incredibly bad in a past life.

Perhaps I was that Roman bloke who played with his instrument while Rome burnt down – Tyrannosaurus rex. Oh no, I don't mean Tyrannosaurus, I mean Nero. If it was Tyrannosaurus rex, that would mean that a dinosaur played a violin, which is clearly not going to happen.

Maybe if I pray for forgiveness and promise to be a better person, Baby Jesus will let me have what I want.

Looking out of my window at the infinite sky, I prayed out, "Dear Baby Jesus, I am sorry for my sins, even though I do not know what they are, which seems a bit unfair if it is going to be held against me.

"But that is your way. And I am not questioning your wisdomosity.

"In future, however, would it be possible for my life to be not so entirely crap? Thank you."

Son of Angus, otherwise Known as Cross-eyed Gordy

Sunday March 13th

I have accidentally come on a nature ramble with my "family". That is how upset I am. And the nature ramble involved getting into the clown car in order to get into nature. This should give you some idea of my state of sheer desperadoes. Vati had his World War Two flying helmet on and his goggles. It was vair vair sad and tragic.

I slumped down in the back of the clown car. I even let Libby make me look "niiiiice". Her idea of looking nice is not the same as most other human beings' (apart from pygmies'). She tied my hair in little pigtails with bits of wool. But I don't care. My life is over and I am a mad toddler's playdough person.

Vati was in an appallingly good mood. When two women

were walking along (practically at the same speed as the clown car), he wound down the window and shouted, "Your big day is here, ladies, the Sex Bomb is officially in his car."

Oh God it was soo humiliating.

I said to Mutti, "I don't think Dad's medication is working, Mum."

2:00 p.m.

Eventually we arrived in "nature", which to some might look like a boring old field in the middle of nowhere. I'd only come to get away from the tension of not answering the telephone. If I had stayed at home and the phone rang, I wouldn't be able to answer it in case it was Dave the Laugh apologising. But then if it didn't ring, I would be indoors waiting all day knowing that he hadn't rung and I hadn't been able to ignore him.

2:20 p.m.

The only bright spot of the day was the sight of Vati jogging off into the fields like a fat mountain goat. I was just sitting in the back of the clown car waiting for my life to be over. Mum and Libby were eating a picnic, Libby in her attractive country costume of furry coat and rabbit hat. Unfortunately I am only too well aware that beneath the furry coat lurks her nuddy-pants outfit. Pray God there will be no poo business in the car.

Dad was cavorting around looking interested in nature, yelling, "Oh my word, there is some cuckoo spit," or "Voles!!" when suddenly he just disappeared from view. Completely gone. I thought about yelling, "Thank you Baby Jesus, it's a miracle!!" But I am still hoping for a bit of a result from the Lord, so I restrained my delight.

Mum got out of the car and tore off across the field shouting, "Bob, Bob, where are you, darling?"

I could hear a muffled yelling. I supposed I had better go and see what had happened to the Portly One. Libbs and I ambled over to where Mum was looking down. And there he was, up to his armpits in a hole.

Even though I am in the depths of despairiosity and so on, it did make me laugh. A LOT. Dad was all red and shouty. "It's a bloody badger hole!!"

That made me go uncontrollably spazoid.

As Mutti pulled him out, he was all grumpy, like the very psychotic get.

"They're a bloody menace, badgers. I am going to inform someone of this. I could have injured myself quite badly. It's not funny."

As Mutti helped him back to the clown car, I said, "I think you should write to someone, Vati, and have badgers banned. While you are at it get beavers banned because they may have been in cahoots with the badgers. They may have encouraged them to dig that hole for a laugh, and—"

"Shut up, Georgia."

Oh that's nice, isn't it. Mutti was inwardly laughing but restrained herself. On the way home she had to drive the clown car because Vati was incontinent. Or do I mean incompetent? Both I think.

At home she made him some tea while he lay groaning and moaning on the sofa.

5:00 p.m.

I was in the kitchen hanging around and Angus was doing his famous staring at the door trick. I'm not falling for it, though. He sits and looks all longingly at the door for ages. Just staring and staring at it. Eventually some poor fool gets up and goes to open it for him. Angus looks out and then he looks at you, then he looks back at the outside. And you can see him thinking, "Nah, I won't bother now."

It's very annoying.

Mum was cutting the crusts off toast for Dad. Which she never does for me. I said to her, "Hey, Mutti, if someone discovers that Vati just floods people's homes as a job, and he gets the sack from the Water Board, he could always get a job as a badger finder. Say you wanted to know where the badgers were in a field... well, you just set Vati off walking and when he disappears from view you know there's a badger there."

Still only 8:00 p.m.

It's so dark and gloomy. Like life. No phone calls.

I HATE Dave the Laugh.

Even though it is very nippy noodles, I can't bear being cooped up in the house. I thought I'd go sit on the garden wall and try to calm down.

I was just sitting there in my big coat and scarf and hat in the street light, looking at all the houses where other people were doing stuff – roasting chestnuts, snogging, etc., when Oscar, Mr and Mrs Across the Road's son, came out on to his driveway on his bike. He was doing wheelies and all that pointless boy stuff that they do: making the bike hop along, braking really suddenly, sitting on the seat backwards and steering it behind his back. All boys are mad as snakes – which is why I must train myself up for lesbianism, even if it involves growing a moustache. If it involved growing a beard under each arm, I was practically home and dry. The orang-utan gene is not having a winter vacation.

Anyway, Oscar saw me watching him and he winked at me. I just looked at him. What is he winking for? Then he winked again. Is he in training for owldom? He shouted over, "Do you fancy it then?"

"Pardon?" I said, "What?"

What is he talking about?

He leant back against his bike and crossed one leg over the other in what I imagine he thinks is a casual way.

He said, "Me and you."

"Me and you what?"

"You know... getting it on."

"Pardon?"

"You know, letting the monster out of the bag, setting free the trouser snake."

I couldn't believe what I was hearing. I said, "Oscar,

101

forgive me if I'm right but you are twelve."

"I know, but I like older women."

Unbelievable. Now I am being propositioned by toddlers. Soon it will be Josh, Libby's little mate from nursery school.

Oscar was still winking at me while I was staring at him when Mark Big Gob came by on his way out. Oh brilliant! He said, "Clear off, Oscar! Bedtime." Oscar looked hard, but he cleared off all the same, saying, "Yeah, well, I was going to go in, I've got a chick phoning me. Dig you later."

Has he gone completely mad?

Mark Big Gob looked at me – or rather, he looked at my nungas.

"You're looking cool, Georgia. Why don't you come for a walk with me Tuesday? I'll be out by the back field at eight o'clock. See you then."

I was just going "What??? What???" in my mind, but nothing was coming out of my mouth.

As if!!! Meet him in the back field???? As if!!!!!

What had happened to his tiny girlfriend??

Anyway, it didn't matter what happened to her. As if I would meet him by the back field or anywhere!

Boys are truly unbelievable.

Monday March 14th
Break

All huddled up in our Antarctic weatherproof tepee behind the five's court. (The Ace Gang get all our coats and button them to each other around us, like a coat tepee.) Mmmm, nice and snug, but it does mean you can't use your arms. We put the snacks in the middle of us inside the coat tepee. You have to eat them blind, grabbing stuff from any bag you can feel and forcing two fingers with the snack in them through the communal neck hole. Tricky if you all try to do it at the same time.

Rosie said, "That was a vair vair good party. I didn't get to bed until eight a.m. and then I had to get up at ten because of my olds coming back."

Ellen said, "I thought your olds were, you know, cool with you having parties."

Rosie said, "Oh they are, it's just that there were a lot of rogue sausage snacks to round up after Sven did his famous 'Let's go down the disco' dance on the cocktail cabinet."

Jools said, "Leslie Andrews is covered in lovebites; she is six inches deep in foundation and she still looks like she has been attacked by lemmings. She tried to wear a polo-neck sweater in Games, but Miss Stamp made her take it off and then tutted for England when she saw the state of her neck."

Oh rave on, who cares about the stupid party? I don't want to talk about it. In a fit of subtlosity I said, "What shall we get as a thoughtful leaving gift for Elvis? Handcuffs? A straitjacket? A T-shirt with 'I am a complete and utter tosser' written on it?"

However, I was *ignorez-vous*ed and Jools said, "You left early, Gee. Why...? Did you have the painters in?"

Jas looked at me. She is still not officially talking to me since the hat over the stupid head scenario.

Everyone looked at me.

Stop looking at me in that lookingy way.

Ellen said, "I am soo upset about Dave the Laugh. I thought he might have got over the thingy, you know, Horn stuff, but then he... you know, brought that girl, you know... er..."

Rosie said, "Rachel."

Ellen said, "No, I'm, I mean I'm Ellen... I you..."

Rosie said, "Ellen, get a grip. The girl, Dave's Horn mate, she's called Rachel."

Ellen went dithering on, "Yes, I mean Rachel. I couldn't believe it when he turned up with her."

I said, "I know."

Ellen was rambling on for England (taking over from Jas, all-time world rambling champion). "I mean, you know, he's supposed to be like a great guy..."

I said, "Yeah... he's supposed to be a great guy but actually he's a snivelling wormy-type guy who leads people on and he... then he..."

Everyone was looking at me (a bit cross-eyed because our heads were so close together). Oh dear, I have slightly blown my glacial disinterest in Dave. I thought quickly. "I mean, it's not fair... on Ellen, is it?"

I said it like I was a great pal. Jas said in her mind, "You skunk girl." So I said telepathically back to her, "Shut up, Wilderness Woman."

Home
6:38 p.m.

The kittykats are going to be sent away!! Mr Across the Road came round, partly to talk about the *Lord of the Rings* party they are going to have. He said, "I'm going as Gandalf and Oscar is thinking about going as a hobbit." Hmm, that's attractive in a twelve-year-old nymphomaniac. I let a smile play around my lips at the thought of my dad in green tights. However, Mr Across the Road – who has taken an unfair dislike to me for some reason – said viciously, "I've found homes for six of those monstrous things, God help the people they are going to, but I can't find anyone stupid enough to have the seventh, so it'll have to go to the vets."

Go to the vets??? I knew what that meant. One of the kittykats was headed for the big cat basket in the sky... After he had lumbered off, Dad settled down on the sofa to read his newspaper. Angus was snoozing in front of the fire.

I said to Dad, "Dad, did you hear that??? Please, please can we save the kittykat: think how upset Angus will be. In fact, I think he understands every word we say and he knows what Mr Across the Road the kittykat abuser said. Look, look, Dad, I think he's crying."

Unfortunately at that moment Angus woke up and leapt straight through the newspaper Dad was reading, tearing it completely in half. Dad got hold of Angus, who also had surprised himself with his insane leap, and flung him across the room. Of course, old nimble paws landed on his feet and ambled off.

Dad was full of lividosity. He said, "Absolutely not in a million years, never, ever, not ever. Do you get it, Georgia, NO."

7:00 p.m.
In the kitchen Mutti was pretending to iron something. I said, "Mutti, that's an iron you know, they can get quite hot."

She said, "Shut up."

In my bedroom
7:15 p.m.
Libby was just doing a spot of housework – she has a handbrush and she brushes and mutters to herself. She was saying, "Bloody thing, bloody thing," as she worked. Obviously gaining her knowledge from my parents. When I lay down on my bed of pain she came and nuzzled me. "Georgia, Georgie Porgy... I LOBE you, kissy kiss kiss."

I wish she had more snot control. I told her, "Angus's kittykats have to go away."

She said, "NO."

I said, "Maybe Mummy will let you have one if you ask her."

Libby gave me a very very scary smile and toddled off with her brush.

I heard her clanking down the stairs singing, "Mummy, Muuuummmmmmeeeeee."

Ten minutes later

I can hear mumbling going on in the kitchen. Libby said, "Nice Muummmeee."

I couldn't hear what Mum was saying but I could tell she was using a reasoning sort of voice.

Then there was banging and shouting. Mutti yelled, "No Libby. Stop that!! No biting and not on my best... Oh hellfire!!"

10:00 p.m.

Our new kittykat is called Gordon. Libby LOBES Gordon very much. She has put him in his pyjamas and tucked him up with me and her other toys. He is very very gorgey but he is a bit on the cross-eyed side.

Gordy is happily sucking on Libby's dodie and all is quiet.

Tuesday March 15th

Gordy woke up at six a.m. and crawled under my chin like a little ginger beard. He is so adorable.

7:00 p.m.

Stalag 14 was indescribably boring today. We had *Blithering Heights* followed by double French. I told the Ace Gang about the absolute cheek of Oscar and Mark Big Gob.

Jas pretended to be giving me her icy shoulders, but even she got interested when I described Oscar looning around trying to get off with me. She said, "Were you wiggling your hips like in the book?"

"Jas, I was sitting down on the wall. Anyway, he's twelve."

She looked all wise-woman-of-the-forestish (i.e. stupid).

"Perhaps you were doing internal hip wiggling."

What is she raving on about?

Still, she is talking to me by mistake and so I win the glaciosity game hahahaha.

7:45 p.m.

I don't know why I have applied make-up to stay in my room.

Mutti and Vati have got Uncle Eddie here and a few of their crap mates. Uncle Eddie popped his head round my door, almost blinding me with the glare from his baldiness. I began to say, "Er, Uncle Eddie, this is a loon-free zone—"

But he said, "What has a hundred legs and can't walk?"

"Uncle Eddie, I am sixteen years old, I—"

"Fifty pairs of trousers... hahahahah it's the way I tell 'em!"

And he looned off to the loon gathering.

I cannot have any peace. I am forced out of my own home because of the high loon count.

7:59 p.m.

I crept out of the house into the back garden. I would just see if Mark Big Gob had the audacity to turn up for our "date". And I could tell him to bugger off.

8:00 p.m.

He's not there. God, even someone I was going to stand up has stood me up before I had a chance to stand them up.

8:02 p.m.

Mark Big Gob came out of the shadows smoking a fag. He

really has got the biggest gob known to humanity. He said, "You're keen."

How annoying is that. I was going to say, "Well, actually I was just here to tell you to bugger off", when he said, "Fancy a fag?"

Er...

I said, "No thanks, I only smoke cigars."

What am I talking about?

He held out his hand.

"Come on then."

I honestly have no control over any part of my body, because even though I had no intention of doing it, I took his hand. Which was a mistake in very many ways. Mostly because I had forgotten that I am taller than him and I have long arms, so I had to do the crouchy orang-utan thing to keep at the same height as him.

Anyway, we loped off up the hill. It was bloody dark and extremely nippy noodles. I had worn my big cardigan, but I still felt a bit chilly because it only buttoned up halfway. Mark is not a big talker and I couldn't think of a single thing to say to him. We got up to the bit at the top we call the bushes – it's really Snog Headquarters. There was no one there tonight, though. Mark let go of my hand and put his fag out. Then he alarmed me by putting his hand round the back of my neck and pulling me to him quite roughly. Blimey. Just as I was deciding what to do he shoved his tongue in my mouth. No warmsy upsies, not even "My your skin is looking nice," or "What a lovely blouse." Not even a nodding acquaintance with one two three four on the snogging scale.

It wasn't that nice actually. His tongue had more than a passing similarity to Angus's. Not that I have snogged Angus, but there has been the odd occasion when he has licked my face and the tongue has inadvertently slipped into my gob. I didn't quite know what to do with my tongue or my teeth. My tongue was sort of being forced back to keep out of the way of his. For one horrible moment I wondered if there was something called "tonsil snogging" that no one had told me about. Mark seemed to be enjoying it even if I wasn't. He was sort of groaning and holding me really close. I was just thinking I might try and get my hands free (they were sort of trapped in between us) when Mark did this thing: he stuck his hand (which was freezing) down the front of my T-shirt and into my nunga-nunga holder.

Number eight, upper-body fondling!! Actually it gave me such a shock that I jumped back and Mark was thrown off balance. He stumbled into the bushes. He came out a minute later covered in twigs. He didn't look pleased.

He said, "What did you do that for?"

I said, "Well. Er, it was all a bit... I don't know that I want you to..."

He lit a fag and said, "What did you come here for... a chat?"

I said, "Well... I..."

What did I come here for? Very good question. Excellent point, well made. Boredom mostly, I suppose. I didn't think I should say that. Mark seemed really angry. He said, "Do you go all the way or not?"

I said, "Well, no I..."

Mark started walking off. "Girls like you make me sick."

And he was gone. I was left at the top of the hill alone. What had I done now? I felt really weird. And lonely.

I walked back down the hill. When I went through our gate, Angus was lying in wait and pounced on my trousers round the ankle. With a heavy heart and even heavier trousers I dragged him indoors.

Midnight

What does Mark mean, "girls like me"?

Wednesday March 16th

Walking to school with Jas.

"Jas, what number have you got up to with Hunky?"

She went all red and girlish. "Er..."

"Come on, Jas, I tell you everything."

Jas said, "I know and I wish you wouldn't."

"Jas."

"Well. Er, when we went camping we, you know, had a bit of quality time together."

"Snogging time you mean?"

"Well yes... we, er, got up to six and a half."

"Ear snogging. Is that all?"

She got huffy then and started adjusting her knickers. "There is more to life than snogging, you know."

I said, "Oh yeah, like what? Going off into the forest snuffling out truffles?"

"Pigs do that."

"Yeah, and your point is?"

Jas said I am being all mean and moody because of Dave

the Laugh, but what she doesn't know is that it's not just Dave the Laugh, it's Oscar, and now Mark Big Gob as well. I feel all ashamed somehow. Like I am tainted love.

Break

Rosie and I managed to escape the Storm Troopers (Wet Lindsay and her pathetico prefect pals). Jas wants to read her book about twig houses, so she has gone off to the five's court with the other girlie swots. Hawkeye insists that we have windows open, even in Antarctic conditions. She says it's good for us but she also says reading absolute bollocks is good for us, so I don't trust her. It is, after all, she who thinks that *Blithering Heights*, as we call it, is a "classic". When in fact it's a load of Yorkshire people hurling themselves around a moor in the wind singing "Heathcliff, it's me Katheeee come home again." And so on. We've only read three pages and already I want to slit my wrists. Anyway, where was I before I so rudely interrupted myself? Oh yes, so because Hawkeye has windows open all over the school, we could get in through the science block window.

Once we got in, we lit a few Bunsen burners for warmth.

Voley is still here in his little pickling jar for ever, waving at us. I said, "Hello, Voley. My dad fell down a badger hole."

I thought he would like to know the news from the forest, even though he has been pickled for years.

Rosie was trying to toast a bit of banana over the naked flame of a Bunsen burner. I sensed a burning-down-the-science-block situation but I didn't want to spoil her girlish high spirits by saying anything. Also, I had just got myself all snuggled up in some science overalls. I decided to tell Rosie about Mark Big Gob.

She listened and said, "He is clearly a knob head, but you knew that. Forget it, we have more important things to think about. There's a lot of work to do at school, and this is a very important term."

I looked at her in amazement. "Rosie, please tell me you are not talking about exams and it's not the way you run the race but the winning that counts."

She gave me the famous cross-eyed look. "Do not be a twit and a fool and a prat. I'm talking about our plans for Mr Attwood's leaving do."

Hockey

I did actually cheer up in Games. There is nothing like socking a bit of concrete about a pitch and smacking shins with my hockey stick to get the juices flowing. Additionally, Nauseating P. Green was goalie, which is a guaranteed laugh. It is funny enough seeing her lumbering around in huge pads picking the ball out of the back of the net, but the *pièce de résistance* was when she fell over on her back and couldn't get up. Like a big tortoise waving her shin pads about. She finally managed to get up after about ten minutes, and just as she was on her feet a ball whizzed in and hit her in the tummy and down she went again.

Cruel, but funny.

Jas's place
5:00 p.m.

Jas and Hunky are going on this wilderness thing soon, so Jas made me go up to her room and look at the stuff she is taking with her. Good grief, the things I do for friendship.

Her room is ludicrously tidy, all her soft toys arranged in size order. Very sad. I said that as I looked around. "Very, very sad."

But Wild Woman of the Forest was too busy rooting around in her wardrobe. She was all enthusiastic. "Look at these. They are my special army-issue waterproof trousers. Even if I, like, accidentally fell into a swamp I would still have dry legs."

I looked at the hideous yellow things. "Are you sure those are not just massive incontinence knickers, Jas?"

She was just rambling on as if I wasn't there, which actually, in my mind, I wasn't.

On and on, completely gone off to Jasland.

"You should get yourself a hobby, Gee, and then you wouldn't end up throwing yourself at boys and losing your dignity."

How annoying is she?

Vair vair and thrice vair annoying.

6:00 p.m.

After about a million years of looking at really dull bits of Wellington boot etc., I slouched off home.

I am so sick of walking. Walk, walk, walk, that's all I ever do. I'll wear my legs out at this rate. To pass the time I did what I used to do as a kid – I pretended to be riding a horse. I galloped along tossing my head about, saying "Giddy-up"

and flicking a pretend whip. The bit between the bottom of Jas's road and my house was very quiet, so I really let my horse (Dark Star) have his head. I flicked at his haunches with my whip and felt the wind on my face and the freedom of the hills. "Yes, yes, ride on my beauty!" I pulled Dark Star to a halt so that we could cross the road, which was just as well, as across the road was Cad of the Universe, Dave the Laugh. Oh brilliant. Thank you, God. My head was practically dropping off from redness and I hadn't any lip gloss on because I had given up on boys.

I crossed the road and walked past him. I treated him with total glaciosity. He said, "Come on, Georgia, talk to me."

"What can you possibly have to say to me?"

I walked on. At least I haven't got ginger hair. Although with my luck, I probably have hair that is sticking out at right angles after my galloping fiasco. As usual, though, Dave kept on. He tends to ignore me ignoring him, which is annoying. He put his arm through mine.

"Georgia, look at me. Come on, Sex Kitty, don't get the megahump. We weren't going out officially, were we? You couldn't make your mind up, then I met Rachel and she was keen... well, she is after all only human—"

I looked at him with a "don't even bother" look. He smiled.

"Can't we be friends? We've always had a laugh together."

I felt my heart melting. He was right, really; we hadn't been officially a couple, and he was a laugh to have around. I found myself going for a coffee with him and telling him all about Mark Big Gob. Dave the Laugh said, "He really is an enormous twit of the first water."

It sort of made it better when he said it. I know that Rosie had said the same, but it seemed different when a boy-type person said it. As we left the coffee bar and walked along arm in arm, he stopped and took my chin in his hand. (I don't mean he snapped it off my face and held it.) He just sort of lifted my face up to his and gave me a little kiss really gently on the lips. I could feel the jelloid knees coming on. Damn!

As I walked off, he called back to me, "Don't worry about Mark Big Gob. I'll have a word."

Home

Oh joy unbounded, Cousin James is coming to stay overnight. I said to Mutti, "Why?"

And she said, "He's family."

I said reasonably, "Mutti, what does that mean? Does it mean that if Hitler was my cousin we would have to have him round?"

She got all parenty. "Now you are being ridiculous. Go and do your homework. Oh, and don't have a bath – Gordy has done a cat poo in there. I'll have to clean it up."

Gordy has done a cat poo in the bath??!! Why would he scramble all the way up the sides of the bath just to do a poo when he has his own personal cat-poo tray in the outhouse? Anyway, how could he get up the sides of the bath? Either Libby gave him a leg up, or Angus helped him. I bet it was Angus. When I went into my bedroom Angus was curled up on my cardigan cleaning himself. I wish he wouldn't do botty grooming on my things. I said to him, "You are quite literally a crap dad, Angus. You wait until Gordy starts staying out all night creating mayhem – you'll be sorry."

Angus fell into a light doze as I was telling him off. Anyway, why would he be worried about Gordy staying out all night creating mayhem? That's what he does himself. It's his job.

9:00 p.m.

Doorbell rang.

No one answered it, of course. Mum and Libby (and I think from the yowling, Angus and Gordy) are all in the bath. I don't know how they can bear to go in there. I personally will never be having another bath in this lifetime, not even if Mum has cleaned it with nitroglycerin.

Ring ring on the bell.

9:03 p.m.

I shouted out, "Don't worry, I'll get it. I've only got exams in two weeks, but you just lie around and relax."

Tramp tramp.

If I get all the way down and it's Cousin James and I have to speak to him I will have a nervy spaz.

9:05 p.m.

I opened the door and it was Mark Big Gob. Crikey. He looked a bit shifty and nervous.

"Georgia, I've got something to say about the other night."

He wasn't going to have another attempt at storming my nunga-nunga holders, was he?

I said warily, "Oh yes. What is it?"

"Well, I'm, I'm..."

I'm what? The Count of Monte Cristo? Stupid? Wearing false lips? What???

Mark said, "I'm sorry. I apologise."

Blimey O'Reilly's trousers. Then I noticed he had a swelling on his mouth and a split lip. Cripes, was his mouth expanding even more, like the Incredible Hulk?

He said, "Do you accept my apology?"

How weird was this? I felt like I was in a film. One of those really old-fashioned films where everyone wears pantaloons. Like *Gone with the Wind*. Maybe I should say, "Why sir, thank you kindly for apprising me of your feelings. I do declare I have never seen tighter pantaloons!!"

But I didn't get into the film thing because Mark is not the brightest button on the cardigan. I said, "Er... yes, well yes."

As he shuffled off, Mark turned round and said, "Will you let your mate know I've been round?"

"What mate?"

"You know, Dave."

Then he went off.

Wow!

And three times wow. In fact wowzee wowzee wow!!!

What had Dave the Laugh done?

9:15 p.m.

Phoned Rosie and told her.

She was very impressed – she loves the smack of violence.

She said, "Hmmm, my kind of guy. It's a good job Sven wasn't involved; a boy at a party I went to pushed into the loo line ahead of me and Sven threw his trousers into next door's garden."

"Why would Sven chuck his trousers into next door's garden? Was it a fit of pique?"

"Georgia, he threw the boy's trousers into next door's garden... and the boy was still wearing them."

"*Sacré bleu.*"

"*Mais oui.*"

9:35 p.m.

In theory, and especially given my special relationship with Jesus, I am against violence. However, there is a time and place for everything, and I think Dave biffing Mark is one of those exceptions that make the rule.

124

9:40 p.m.
It slightly gives me the Horn, actually.

Unlike Cousin James, who unfortunately has arrived. He is reading Tolkien's *The Hobbit* and goes on and on about it.

He said, "It's very interesting, but did you know that even now people go on a pilgrimage to Tolkien's grave and they speak in Elfin?"

James has a bit of trouble with the word "interesting". In fact, sad sacks chatting in Elfin over some dead bloke's grave is not "interesting", it is "stupid".

Still, at least he is reading rubbish and not trying to play tickly bears with me.

Midnight
What is it with boys and elves?

Thursday March 17th
Phoned Dave the Laugh and thanked him *vis-à-vis* the duffing-up incident. He said, "It's a pleasure, gorgeous."

But he didn't say "see you later" or anything.

Saturday March 19th

At one time I had boys snogging my ears and so on, and now I am alone for the rest of my life. How did that happen? How come I have peaked already?

11:00 p.m.
Started a letter to SG:

Dear Robbie,
   It's raining here and we are doing a crap play about some Scottish fools who...

11:15 p.m.
I can't talk about school to him, otherwise he will remember that I am still at school.

Friday April 1st, All Fools Day

You are not kidding.

Friday April 8th

I have tried to write to Robbie so many times, but the sadness is that I don't have anything to say to him. He doesn't want to be my boyfriend and I just have to accept it.

I am going to take down my shrine to him.

11:00 p.m.
Mum came in after I had taken down my shrine and she caught me crying.

She sat down on the edge of the bed and stroked my hair, which is normally a killing offence, but it was all scrubbled up and greasy anyway. She said, "I'm sorry, love, I'm sorry you're so upset, but you will have fun again and you will have nice boyfriends because you are lovely and funny and my darling daughter."

That made me cry more.

Then Libby toddled in and came up on the bed beside me.

"Look, Ginger, nice."

She had what I think was probably once a biscuit in one hand and Gordy by the neck in the other. She put him on my bed and he started attacking my knees under the bedclothes.

Midnight

Mum made me a milky pops drink like she did when I was little and ill. Which was nice. Except that I put it down on my bedside table and Gordy plunged his head in it. He has been having a sneezing attack for about ten minutes.

Snog factor 25 and a half

Monday April 11th
School

Hot news straight off the press: The Stiff Dylans have got a new lead singer to replace the Sex God. Ellen was full of it in the loos. We were all holed up there at break. If any Storm Troopers come in we have to stand on the loo seat so they can't see our feet. The trick is to leave the door a bit open and stand right to the other edge of the loo seat, so the cubicle looks empty. We are clearly geniuses, because it works.

Anyway, Ellen said, "He's half Italian and half American and he's called Masimo."

Jools said, "I'm going to learn how to speak American immediately."

"Mabs reckons he's dishy and fit as a flea."

"Angela Richards saw him arrive at the Phoenix. She lives just across from it and she said he turned up on one of those really cool Italian scooters."

11:00 a.m.

I listened to their girlish chatter with great sadnosity. It was all right for them; they could just replace one lead singer with another. They did not know the heartbreak I had gone through because the Sex God had chosen wombats and rogue bores instead of me.

Jools said, "Angela said he is the coolest, fittest-looking boy she has ever seen. When he drew up and was parking his scooter this group of girls sort of gathered around just looking. Ogling him. He said *ciao* to them."

I said, "How is he going to be able to be in the band if he can't speak English?"

Ellen said, "He can speak English, he's half American."

I said, "Oh yeah, and that's the same, is it? I'll just say this – Americans don't know who Rolf Harris is, and they call knickers 'panties'. That is not really speaking English, is it?"

Rosie said, "Yeah, you've got a point, Geegee, but perhaps

in the spirit of neighbourliness and red-bottomosity we could help him to speak properly."

Hmmm.

Swimming

Herr Kamyer was "in charge" this arvie because Miss Stamp was doing some certificate or other.

I said, "It's probably in advanced lesbianism."

It probably is, actually.

In the pool

I swam under Jas's legs and she squealed like a girl because I surprised her.

She was very grumpy because in her panic she had got her fringe wet.

My crawl style is quite stylish I think. Unlike Nauseating P. Green's style. She really is a fiasco waiting to happen. She wears armbands and she still sinks without a trace every few minutes.

Anyway, the funniest bit for me was when Herr Kamyer entered stage left. He came out in his swimming knickers and we all went, "Phwoaar," which made him have such a dither attack that he stepped off into the deep end by mistake. Without removing his glasses. He spent about a million years diving down to look for them. Herr Kamyer is the palest man known to humanity. His legs and arms are like a stick insect. He does a very amusing breaststroke (in my opinion) like a cross between a human being and a twit, with just a touch of blind beaver. I could watch him for ages.

We were all having splashy fun when the fire alarm went off. Oh *merde*! Now what? It couldn't be a real fire, and even if it was, wouldn't we be better off staying in forty-five million gallons of water, like where we already were?

But oh no, that would be too simple. The lifeguard was Mr Attwood. He came perving along with a whistle and started yelling at us to get out of the water and go to our mustering points. What mustering points? What are we, bucking broncos?

I said to RoRo as we dragged ourselves up the swimming pool steps, "I can't believe this!"

When we tried to go and get changed, Elvis had locked the doors to the changing rooms. He said, "Come on, come on, follow the exit signs pronto."

Rosie, who was practically hitting Mr Attwood in the spectacles with her nungas, said, "Yes, but where do the signs lead?"

And he said, "Outside to safety. Now get a move on."

"Outside??"

Minutes later we were outside, in early April, in the car park. In our semi-nuddy-pants.

We were shivering like mad when Mr Mad came round with some BacoFoil stuff. I said to him, "This is hardly the time to be roasting vegetables."

And he, in a rather surly way for someone who was supposed to be calming me down in the face of a towering inferno, said, "It's to wrap around you."

Marvellous.

Thank you.

3:00 P.M.

I will not easily forget standing in a car park wrapped in BacoFoil next to Herr Kamyer, also in BacoFoil.

He was still trying to be normal. Not that he has the slightest idea what that is, as he is German.

He said, "So girls, shall we sing a little song to practise

our German? I know, let us do the funny camping one of when the Koch family go away and they forget many things which we must list."

God save us all.

Saturday April 16th

Jas has gone off to the Forest of Fools with Hunky, so the rest of the Ace Gang went to Churchill Square for essential shopping items. It's incredibly nippy noodles and parky, but that didn't stop us casually sitting on a wall chatting and lad spotting. There were hordes of lads ladding about. There is an all-nighter at the Buddha Lounge tonight, but unfortunately since my report card I am virtually under house arrest. It's a lot of fuss over nothing. Slim said on the "remarks" part of my report card, "Georgia is an intelligent girl whose academic career is blighted by her immature japes."

"Immature japes". Lawks a mercy! I bet when Slim went to school they used to make their own fun with bits of old Weetabix packets. And a really great night out was going down the grocers and thinking about what you could make with dairy products. But tragically, life is not like that. We do not do "immature japes", we do really sophisticated japes.

Just as we were reapplying lippy after our nutritious lunch of choc-ices, Dave the Laugh and Rollo came along. When they saw us, Dave said, "Be gentle with us."

What was he going on about? Ellen practically exploded with ditherosity. I, on the *au contraire*, was a visage of casualosity. I even remembered to smile with my tongue behind my back teeth. Dave winked at me. Shut up winking.

Rollo was looking all sheepish. I think he still likes Jools, even though he finished with her. Jools is keen but she's playing hard to get. Ellen has obviously taken my hints from our boy bible on "how to make any fool fall in love with you" seriously. She was flicking her hair around so much I thought she might snap her neck. And also she was combining it with darting glances. Dave said, "All right, Ellen?"

And she said, flickyflick, "Yes, I'm all right, Dave. Are... you... all right?" And she gave a very meaningful flick and darting glance. But no one got it.

As I was being a bit reddish, Dave's so-called girlfriend turned up. She is not pretending to be reddish, she IS reddish. Good grief she's friendly. She said, "Oh hi, everyone, great to see you again."

135

Was it? Why? Before I knew it we were all pretending to be really jolly and friendly for no reason. It was very very tiring. After they had gone, Jools and Rollo were talking to each other "privately", so Rosie and Ellen and me went to try out make-up in Boots. When Ellen went round the other side of the "Rich Chick" range, I said to Rosie, "Rachel's a bit like Jas, isn't she, only more ginger. It's all 'ooohhh look, some cuckoo spit' and 'ooooh have a nice day' and 'ooooh your hair is nice' and—"

Rosie said, "Yes I think I've got the picture, Gee, and I think you are being very bitter and twisted and that's why I *aime* you so much."

I thought Ellen was busy trying on flavoured eye shadow (a bit of a mystery that one, unless there is such a thing as eye snogging, which quite frankly wouldn't surprise me). Anyway, Ellen popped her head up really suddenly and said, "You are not very nice about Dave the Laugh, Georgia. I mean, I am, and I'm the one he... well, you know, I'm the dumpee. Not you. I mean, what has he ever done to you? You know that time when you were supposed to snog him at the fish party, well..."

I started blabbing about my mates being like part of me.

Fortunately at that point Jools came running over like an excitable elephant in a frock.

"He says he'd like to give it another go."

We spent the rest of the afternoon arguing about whether you should give a boy a second chance.

Who knows, the whole thing is a bloody mystery.

Home

I am under heavy manners this weekend, even to the extent that I am being forced to stay in and baby-sit whilst the so-called grown-ups go out and make fools of themselves. The rest of the Ace Gang are going to the funfair. I tried saying to Vati that we had been set "going to the funfair" as homework, but all he said was, "Georgia, let me put it this way... No."

Mutti said, "Anyway, you're baby-sitting for us. It's Uncle Eddie's birthday and we're going out."

They are going to some really sad karaoke bar. Uncle Eddie won first prize the last time singing "Like a Virgin", so that should give you some idea about how crap it must be.

Mutti was tarting herself up in the bathroom. She said, "Honestly, when he started singing 'Like a Virgin' it was like Madonna was there in his body."

Christ, what an image.

As a fabulous parting gift, Mum said, "Oh, by the way, I've made an appointment to see Dr Gilhooley. Put it in your diary."

I said, "Oh no. No, no, no, there is nothing wrong with me that having normal parents wouldn't fix. I will not show him my elbows again. They're fine, I'm living with them."

Mutti said, "It's not about your health. I just want to see him because he's so gorgeous."

She saw me looking sick and said, "No, not really. I want to fix up a work experience day for you there. I know how much you like biology."

"What???? What??? Just because I can do a fantastic impression of a lockjaw germ does not mean I want to be a doctor's receptionist."

"It'll be interesting. It will give you a taste of real life."

"Mum, you've been in his surgery, you know it's not a taste of real life, it's a taste of pensioner hell. I am not sitting around all day in a place full of people like Mr Next Door in incontinence trunks."

I may as well be invisible, because she just went out tutting.

7:50 p.m.

After Mutti and Vati had roared off in the clown car – or Robinmobile, as I call it – I went up to see what my little sister was up to. She is obsessed with Gordy and is trying to teach him to jump through her hula hoop. Good luck, mad toddler. It's not that Gordy can't leap, he can – in fact he leaps all the time for no apparent reason. But it is senseless leaping, not hoop leaping.

8:00 p.m.

Gordy is so alarmingly cross-eyed, it may be that he can't even see the hoop. I wonder if you can get cat glasses?

Angus is not in. He's on the wall with Naomi snogging and wrestling. It's a bit pervy snogging in front of your offspring. I should know – my olds are always fondling each other and it's disgusting. There is some manky big black cat from up the road hanging about. I see him around Naomi sometimes; he is a rival for her love.

Naomi is a dreadful minx; she seems to entice Manky, even in front of Angus. She is the furry-faced shame of womanhood.

8:25 p.m.

Oh *quel dommage*, Gordy is wrestling with his own tail and the tail is winning, so Libby has turned her attention to me. Oh dear.

"Gingey, let's go play outside now."

"Darling, it's nearly bedtime. I know... we could read *Heidi*."

That's when the *Heidi* book hit me quite hard on the head. Libby had apparently gone off cheese and lederhosen. She was stamping her little foot.

"Outside, naughty boy... OUTSIDE!"

Oh hell's biscuits.

And she wouldn't even get dressed. I had to put a blanket over her jimmyjams (at least she had the bottoms on, for once). She was leaping around, yelling, "Hickory dickory dot, the cow leapt over the SPOOOOON!!"

I opened the front door and she went leaping out into the dark night. Angus looked down at us from the wall and casually biffed me with his paw. Thanks for your help, furry pal. When we got to the gate I said to Libbs, "There, that was nice leaping, wasn't it? Let's go back to snuggly buggly bed and—"

But she had undone the gate and was leaping away down the street in her blanket. I went after her and tried to pick her up. She nearly had my eye out.

8:40 p.m.

Ten minutes later we were still leaping "over the spoon". My plan was to leap with her and sort of round her up and head her back to our house. But I'd just get her in the right direction and she would do some quick leaps and get round me again. By this stage we had got halfway down Baron's Street, and when I looked up from another failed attempt to head Libby off I saw Dom from The Stiff Dylans getting out of his van with his guitar. Probably turning up for a jamming session at the Phoenix. Libby was leaping in a circle, so I had a chance to smile at Dom.

He said, "Hey, hi, how are you, Georgia. And Libby."

Libby ignored him because she was busy leaping. But she still managed to tell him, "Gordon pooed in the bath."

Dom said, "I won't even ask. Have you heard from Robbie?"

I felt a bit tearful. "Yeah, he really likes it there."

Dom said, "Yeah. I heard. Pity. Ah well... erm, come to the gig on the eighth. We've re-formed and got a cool new singer, so it looks like the record deal might go ahead."

I said, "You've got a new singer. Yes, well, that's cool..."

I was thinking, *Yes, that is cool if you can replace a Sex God, which you can't, even if he is a bit obsessed with vegetables.* But I didn't say that.

A silver scooter tore round the corner and stopped outside the Phoenix.

Dom said, "This is him actually – Masimo."

So, at last, this was the so-called Italian-American pseudo Sex God. Huh. How interested was I out of ten? Minus twelve. Unfortunately Libby was interested in the noise of the scooter, and also because it had mirrors and stuff on it. She went leaping over to the scooter.

I yelled, "Libby, come back here now!"

One word from me and she does as she likes. I could hear her saying to the new singer, who was bending over taking off his helmet, "Heggo, I am a moo cow."

Oh bloody Blimey O'Reilly.

I went and got hold of her round the arms, pinning them down so that she couldn't hit me, and lifted her up. But with an alarming change of mood she started kissing me really wildy all over my hair and face. She was ruffling my hair up and messing up my lip gloss. Very very annoying and wet.

"I LOBE you, my Ginger."

I hadn't actually looked at the pretend Sex God as I was busy trying to wrestle with Libby, but then he spoke with an accent that was quite Italian.

"Hello, Ginger. And *ciao*, little moo cow."

I looked at him. Ohmygiddygodstrousers! He was absolutely gorgeous. Really really gorgey. Really gorgey! And I do mean gorgey. That's why I said it. He had very black wavy hair and a tan – a tan in England in April. And he had eyes and teeth and a mouth. He had a back, front, sides, arms, everything. His mouth wasn't as big as Mark Big Gob's (whose was?) but it was on the generous side. And he had really long eyelashes and AMBER eyes. In fact he had eyes like someone I knew, and then I realised he had eyes like Angus. How freaky deaky!! They were the same colour as Angus's! But they didn't have that casual madnosity that Angus's had. In fact they were smiley and soft and dreamy.

Then I realised that about two hundred years had passed since he had said hello.

I forced Libby's mouth off the back of my neck (in a loving and caring way). I thought, *Act natural and normal, do not under any circumstances have an uncontrollable laughing attack.* I took a deep breath. "Ah yes well, er *ciao* to you too. I'm not really ginger, it's just a trick of the light. Hahahahahahaha."

Oh brilliant, I was having an uncontrollable laughing attack.

Dom must have realised that my brain had dropped out because he said, "Masimo, this is Georgia. Georgia, this is Masimo, our new lead singer. Georgia was, erm, friendly with Robbie."

Masimo. Masimo. Whohoa Masimo! I must get a grip. Masimo was locking up his scooter. He looked up and looked me straight in the eye. I managed not to fall over. He said, "Well, Georgia, it was really nice to meet you. I hope we meet again. *Ciao.*"

Then they walked off to go into the Phoenix.

I said, "Yes, *ciao.*"

And Libby shouted, "Night-night, botty boy!"

I turned round and carried her off as fast as I could.

"Libby, why did you say that naughty thing? Don't say it again!"

Libby was singing, "Have you seen the botty boy, the botty boy, the botty boy..."

Where does she get all this stuff from?

God, she weighs a lot these days. I was exhausted when we finally got home. I tucked her up in her bed – she didn't want to come into my bed because she was cross with me for yelling at her. She wouldn't even give me a good-night kiss, although she did manage a quick whack round my ear with scuba-diving Barbie.

In bed

Good grief.

The Dreamboat has landed again.

Midnight

Now I've really got the Cosmic Horn. The only fly in the armpit is that he hasn't shown the slightest interest in me.

12:35 a.m.

Although he did say, " I hope we meet again."

But does it mean that he hopes we meet again, or, you know, like he hopes we meet again but not really?

Oh happy days, I am on the rack of love again.

Monday April 18th
Stalag 14

Had to try to apply make-up on the move because I woke up so late. So there was a mascara-brush-in-the-eye incident. Jas was all fresh faced by her gate. And ludicrously cheerful. And loud.

"Hi, Georgia, look, I've got my Wilderness badge. I've put it next to my Rambler's badge. Do you see? Great, isn't it?"

"Jas, something really—"

"Well, when we got there we had to construct a shelter out of branches and Tom—"

"Jas, I don't want to hear about your twig house. I want to tell you about Mr Gorgeous."

Jas said, "You know the Ace Gang rule."

"What Ace Gang rule?"

"She who starts first must be heard."

"Yes, but it was ages ago we made that rule... and anyway, you are just going to rave on about twigs whereas I want to tell you about this gorgey—"

But Jas had her hands over her ears and was humming. Oh my giddy aunt's brassiere.

I mouthed at her, "OK, you start."

She gave me a scary smile. "Are you sure you're interested?"

I felt like yelling, "Of COURSE I'm not interested, you complete twit!!" But I smiled back and said, "Of course I am, go on, tell me about making a nourishing stew out of bits of old turnip and badger poo."

She looked all stroppy.

"You're not really interested."

"I am."

"You're not, otherwise you would ask an intelligent question."

Oh dear God.

"Oh OK, er, did Tom's Swiss Army knife come in handy?"

"Ah well, it's funny you should say that because..."

8:50 a.m.

Three million years later she finished her ludicrously boring ravings on, by which time we had arrived at Stalag 14. Hawkeye – not world renowned for her deep love of me – was eyeing me like a mad beagle.

"Georgia Nicolson, you are covered in make-up, you look like a creature of the night. Go and take it off immediately, and also take a bad conduct mark."

I was grumbling to Jas as we slouched off. "Creature of the night, what is she going on about?"

As I came out of the loo to scamper off to assembly with that lovely red scrubbed look so beloved by the very sad, I bumped into Wet Lindsay.

"Georgia Nicolson, you are three minutes late for assembly. Take a bad conduct mark."

I said, "I tell you what, Lindsay, why don't you just boil me in oil and call it a day?"

But I said it after she had trolloped off on her extremely knobbly legs.

English

We are doing the life of the Bard of Avon, otherwise known as Billy Shakespeare or the Swan of Avon, as Rosie calls him, because she deliberately misheard "bard" as "bird". Miss Wilson was raving on about his doublet and how he invented language.

Oh I am sooo bored, and distracted by my new pash, Masimo. I can't stop thinking about him. He is by far the dreamiest boy in the universe and probably beyond.

I sent a note to Rosie and said to pass it on to all of the gang. I wrote it in Shakespearean-type language, because I can't help being artistic. And also I have a thirst for knowledge(ish).

I wrote: Odds bodkin I am boredeth. I feeleth a let us goeth down ye olde discotheque coming on.

Rosie wrote back: Forsooth and lack a day let us grooveth!!

So when Miss Wilson turned her back to write something dull on the blackboard, we had a quick burst of manic "Let's go down the disco" dancing to relieve our girlish tension.

Vair vair *amusant*.

Break

Miss Wilson will be very pleased with Billy's enduring effect on the culture of England. When Rosie sat on the knicker toasters in the Blodge labs, she leapt up and said, "Lawks a mercy, I burneth my bum-oley!"

Which made me laugh a LOT. I think I may be hysterical with love.

I don't know whether to tell the Ace Gang about Masimo. They might think wrongly that I am a superficial sort of person who leaps from Sex God to Sex God.

I decided to keep my love news extravaganza for the lugholes of my one and only bestest pal, Jas.

School gates
4:00 p.m.

I couldn't wait to tell her, but I had to because she was droning on and on to the rest of the gang at the gates about her slug-eating weekend. On and on. I may have dropped off for a minute, because she had to say, "Come on then, Georgia, don't you want to get away from this place?"

As we ambled along, I started telling Jas about Masimo.

"He is beyond gorgey, Jas – really really *bon* and also *formidable* in the extreme. He's got these eyes, you know, really fab, like Angus's eyes only, you know, great. Also he has got snog factor twenty-five and a half."

"I thought the snogging scale only went up to ten."

"Jas, pay attention. I said snog factor – that means like sex appeal."

"Why haven't I been told about the snog factor thing."

"Look, Jas, I just made it up and—"

"Well, why have a rule if you are just going to break it and make up your own stuff? It would be like if we were in the wilderness camp and it said to make your own fire and someone used matches."

Oh God, I couldn't believe we were back here again,

round the sodding campfire. I said, "Anyway, he is fabby beyond the dreams of avarice. I have got all of the Horns combined for him: Particular, General and Cosmic."

Jas looked very disapproving. "You said Robbie was your only one and only only one and now it's Masimo, who you've only seen for two minutes. You will end up a lonely person with a reputation for promiscuosity."

What is the matter with her? She is the Mother Teresa for a new generation, with a crap fringe. I was furious. I said, "Yes, but do you know what the good news is, Jas? I won't end up YOU, Mrs Slug Eater."

She got the megahump and we were walking along *ignorez-vous*ing each other when we came across Dave the Laugh AGAIN. Since he got a girlfriend I've seen him all the time; I wonder if he's stalking me. I was about to say that when he grinned and said, "Look, Georgia, stop following me around, you know I love it."

Damn!! By this time we had reached Jas's gate and she went into her drive and said, as a parting shot, "Georgia thinks Masimo is really cool. She likes him, if you know what I mean."

I couldn't believe it!! She had ratted on me and cheapened

my love by announcing it on Radio Jas. I could feel my ears going red. As we walked on, Dave was looking at me in a looking-at-me way. Which I hate.

"You just can't resist a lead singer, can you, Georgia? He's flash."

I said, "He's not flash, he's Italian, that's what they're like."

Dave said, "When I saw him, he was carrying a handbag."

"That's not a handbag, that's a... er... wallet thing."

"It's a bag he carries in his hand, known as a handbag."

I said quickly, not necessarily bothering to involve my brain in the process, "He keeps his revolver in it."

Dave looked right into my eyes. He said, "Excuse me – are you officially mad?"

I said, "No, are YOU mad?"

And he went, "No... are YOU mad?"

We'd got to my gate by then and we could have gone on with the "No, are YOU mad?" game for ever, but as I started my bit Dave stopped me by tickling me in the ribs. It made me splutter and I got spazoid and he kept doing it. Now I was playing tickly bears with Dave the Laugh. He'd probably start talking Elfin in a minute. What is the matter with boys? I said to Dave, "What in the name of arse is the matter with boys?"

And he looked at me and then just snogged me! How dare he!!! I tried to tell him off but I couldn't speak for the snogging. I don't like to admit this under the circumstances, but he really is a cool snogger and I forgot everything in the puckerosity of the moment. When we stopped for breath he said, "Phwoar – excellent snogging, Georgia."

I said, "Why did you do that? You're going out with someone else."

Dave said, "So?"

I said, "Well, it's not right."

"What isn't?"

"You enticing me and snogging me when you're going out with someone else."

"Georgia, you're repeating yourself, and anyway, there's an explanation."

Oh here we go. He'll tell me that it's really me he likes and that it's *moi* he wants, but I'll have to say, "I'm sorry, Dave, but I'm putting you aside with a firm hand – I am in love with another."

I looked at him sympathetically. "What is the explanation, Dave?"

"I like snogging you and I have got the General Horn."

"But..."

"It's my age. I'll grow out of it when I'm about forty-five."

"But I..."

"Don't you like snogging me?"

"Well, that's not the point, I mean, don't you like Rachel...?"

"Yeah, she's cool, but I like you as well, and come to think of it, I quite fancy your mum."

"You fancy my mum????"

I couldn't believe my earlugs! Actually, I think even Dave felt like he had gone that little bit too far. He said, "It's nothing personal, it's just my hormones. Tell them off."

I just looked at him.

He said, "Look, girls and boys are different. Girls like to be touched twenty times a day in a nonsexual way to feel good about themselves – that's why I tickle you and link arms with you – but boys think about sex, snogging and football, and also snogging whilst playing football. Simple."

Home

No one in.

I am completely and utterly living in a state of confusiosity.

Dave is clearly insane.

But what if he's right?

Actually, the way he describes it, it explains a lot of things – Oscar, Mark Big Gob, Cousin James, and those boys from Foxwood that run into our legs and say, "Any chance of a shag?"

5:00 p.m.

But on the other hand, what about Hunky with boring old Jas, and Sven and Rosie? Oh, I don't know.

5:05 p.m.

Also, I sometimes get the Cosmic Horn, so does that mean I'm half girl, half boy?

5:30 p.m.

Does that mean I will have periods and also be heavily bearded and good at reading maps?

Actually, looking at my legs, I suspect I do have a touch of the hermaphrodite about me. When does the hair do its growing? It wasn't there this morning and now it's about a foot long.

5:45 p.m.

Mutti came in from work. I looked at her. How could Dave the Laugh say he quite fancied her? I wonder if she fancies him. Probably – she has no moral backbone. Ohohohoh get out of my head!!!

6:00 p.m.

The phone rang and for once Mutti answered it. She started giggling. "So, it's like a sort of dance orgy thing?" Then I heard her going, "No!!" Then more silence... "No!!!... and he took off all his clothes... to the music??"

Good Lord.

Then Mum began again, "Uh-huh... no... no... no... No!!!"

I thought I would have to kill her to stop her, and then she started again, "So does everyone get naked? Oh I see... he just spontaneously took everything off because he'd got carried away by the music. Wow! What time does it start? OK, what are you wearing? OK, see you there."

Bedroom

The world, which once seemed a simple place, has gone mad. Mutti has gone off to dance with men in their nuddy-pants. She says it's called "Five Rhythms". I bet. Dad is out with his ludicrous mates in the Robinmobile, probably marauding around harassing women. Libby is destroying some poor fool's house. She has taken Gordy round in his cat basket to "wisit" Josh. I don't think that Gordy was specifically invited. Even Angus is off in his luxury bachelor pad with Naomi; he's back in the Prat Poodles' kennel because Mr and Mrs Next Door are out.

6:30 p.m.
I will have to try to distract myself from thinking about Masimo and the whole Cosmic Horn thing. I'll try doing some homework. Another bad conduct mark and it's Detention City for me.

6:45 p.m.
How boring is *Blithering Heights*? Remind me never to read anything else by Emily Brontëchitis.

7:00 p.m.
I am soooo restless.

Phoned Jools and Ellen and they said they would meet me at "homework club", which is our code for the clock tower.

8:00 p.m.

It's incredibly nippy noodles but at least my face is snug. It should be – it has several layers of make-up on it. I've got so much mascara on I'm going to have to do eyelid exercises to keep my eyes open. We sat on the wall by the Co-op. Mark Big Gob came by with his unusually lardy mates, but to my absolute amazement he said, "All right?" to me. Which is the nearest thing to him saying, "Good morrow, Miss Nicolson."

Jools and Ellen were totally fazed. Jools said, "He acted almost like a human being."

We discussed the mystery that is boydom. Jools is still thinking about whether to go out with Rollo again. She said, "The last time, he finished with me because he wanted his freedom – so will he want it again in a week, when we start going out again?"

Hmmmmm.

I said, "I'm going to have to read more of my *How to Make Complete Fools Fall in Love with You* book.

Ellen said, "You said the book said that if I danced by myself, Dave the Laugh would come and get off with me. He got off, but not with me... so what the book says is rubbish."

I said, "The book didn't have a chapter called 'Dance by

Yourself, Ellen, and Dave the Laugh Will Get Off with You'. It just said that it was a way of enticing boys into your web. And someone did come and dance with you, just not the right someone."

Sometimes I amaze myself with my wisdomosity.

As we walked along, we happened to pass by the Phoenix. (Well, when I say "happened" to pass what I mean is that I deliberately wandered that way.) There was a light on and The Stiff Dylans' van was outside. Wow... trembly and jelloid knees.

I said, "I bet Masimo is in there. You know, the new singer with the Dylans. He is absolutely groovy and marvy and fab."

Jools said, "So you quite rate him then?"

I said, "There's a stage door sort of thing that you can get in, and we could have a look at him and the Dylans rehearsing. Come on, it'll be cool."

Ellen was having a dither attack and talking rubbish about private property and so on. But she followed me and Jools round the back in the dark to the stage door. It was open, so we quietly went in. We could hear the band playing. The door to the main club room was straight ahead, but to the right was a room that they used as a dressing room. I'd been in it for snogging extravaganzas with Robbie. Thinking of him made me feel a bit wobbly, but he had chosen furry freaks called wombats rather than me; I had to think of the future. We opened the door and I said to Jools and Ellen, "There's a gap at the top of the wall from where you can see right on to the stage. We could step up on this chair and then on to those boxes."

My skirt was so tight that I had to tuck it into my knickers to get up. Jools said, "Now I have quite literally seen everything."

Ellen wouldn't get up because she was a scaredy cat. Either that or she was wearing something alarming in the pants department. She has probably been studying at the Jas school of big knickers.

It was so exciting. When we got up there we could see right on to the stage and no one could see us – the boy stalkers.

Oh general jelloidosity... there they were, the lads. And one lad in particular. Masimo was wearing a groovy Italian shirt and jeans. He was singing "Play Cool" and it sounded marvy with a bit of an accent.

Jools whispered, "Phwoar."

And I said, "I know."

After a few minutes they stopped playing and Dom said, "Shall we pack it in for now? I'm starving."

Masimo said, "Yeah, I think it is... how you say... kicking? Do you like to come round to my house and I will fix us some pasta and vino?"

Dom said, "*Ciao bella, mon amigo.*"

And they all laughed and started packing up their gear. Masimo said, "Oh damn... *Scusi*, first I make a phone call."

Ben said, "Hot date, Masimo?"

Masimo smiled – good grief, he was sex on a dish when he smiled. "Well... it's just someone, she... I will tell her another night. It is cool."

He jumped off the stage. Oh God's shortie nightie, he might come into the dressing room... and although I was keen, I thought being found on a box practically in your nuddy-pants seemed just that little bit too keen.

We scrambled down, nearly killing Ellen, and rushed off to the door and outside.

11:00 p.m.

I had to run home to make sure I got back into Gestapo Headquarters before the olds returned. *Pant pant pant.*

Masimo was *pant pant* gorgey... but who was the girl on the phone *pant pant*?

Angus was just strolling home with a mouse tail, as a special present for Mutti. How pleased she will be. I raced upstairs and leapt into bed to dreamy dream how to entrance Masimo.

Perhaps I had better learn Italian.

I may suggest to Slim that I give up German because there's no chance I'll be going there ever since I learnt that snogging in German is *knutschen*. And as that would leave a gap in my school schedule, I could learn Italian instead because I have a deep interest in er... ancient Rome and so on.

Tuesday April 19th
Jas's house

Jas must be setting off at dawn to get to Stalag 14 because she was there before me. She is trying to *ignorez-vous* me, because I called her Mrs Slug Eater.

Maths

I gave Jas my most attractive smile but she pretended she was interested in quadratic equations.

Break

Absolutely typical of this bloody place. I went to see Slim about my Italian plan and I didn't even get to the ancient Rome bit. In fact, to be honest, I didn't even get to her office. Hawkeye asked me why I was hanging around waiting to see Slim, and I explained my interest and she said, "Don't annoy me any more than you do simply by turning up to school. Off you go."

That's nice and encouraging isn't it? I don't know why she's a teacher; she hates us. Oh no, I tell a lie – she likes all the useless girlie wet beaky swots like Wet Lindsay and Astonishingly Dim Monica and so on.

Lunchtime

I borrowed an Italian book from the library, *Parliamo Italiano*, and found a comfy loo, put my feet up and read.

Five minutes later

Constantly disturbed by ludicrously excited first formers chasing each other and saying, "Oh we did something really brilliant in Blodge – we looked at pond life under a microscope." Surely I wasn't like them at their age.

Christ, now they are playing tig. Well, they were until Wet Lindsay came in to torture them. Of course, she came rattling at my study door.

"Who's in there?"

"It's me."

"Who's me?"

"I am."

She completely and unreasonably lost her rag.

"Get out here now!"

Oh odds bodkin. I sloped out of the loo. She was remarkably red, and there is really no excuse for her knees.

"I might have known it would be you."

I said, "Lindsay, forgive me if I'm right, but there is no law against going to the piddly-diddly department, is there?"

She said, "Don't be so cheeky."

I didn't bother to reply. As I was leaving, she said, "Off you go and play with your silly playmates. Honestly, when will you lot grow up?"

I really hate her. She has never forgiven me for going out with Robbie, or for when she fell over into the sanitary dispenser when I was trying to help her in the school panto.

Outside

Brrrr. I found a little sheltered corner round the back of Elvis's hut. The old maniac was nowhere to be seen. So I snuggled under my coat to learn about the Pasta-a-gogo people.

Blodge

Rosie said, "Where in the name of Slim's chins have you been all lunchtime?"

I told her about my Italian studies. "The main nub and thrust of their gorgey language is that you add 'o' to everything."

She said, "Oh, OK, what is... er... 'desk' then?"

"Deskio."

She looked at me. "What is 'snog'?"

"Snoggio."

I think she was quite impressed.

4:15 p.m.

No sign of Jas. She must be running like the wind when the bell goes, or lurking around until she sees me going home. She is so childish.

Home
5:30 p.m.

Mutti insisted on taking me to Dr Clooney's surgery. She has made an appointment with him to talk about my work experience. The whole thing is a fiasco. Jas is going to work in the Jennings's fruit and veg shop, which means she will be snogging Tom, and Rosie says her work experience will be "having the flu", and so that means her work experience will be snogging Sven. I don't know why everyone is bothering with all this work business. I have set my sights far higher than having a job. I am going to be a pop star's girlfriend. It's hard work, but someone has to do it. Try telling that to my mum, though. I did try actually. I said, "Look, Mum, it's pointless going to find out about jobs and stuff, because I am going to be rich beyond the beyond of the Universe of Beyond."

She was trying to capture Gordy and Libby, and was getting quite bad-tempered.

"Oh yes, and how are you going to do that, exactly?"

"I have a plan."

"Does it involve hanging around with someone in a local band and them getting a record deal and then you living in a luxurious flat in London and America and having anything you want, for ever and ever? Is that your plan?"

Wow, sometimes she is almost psychic. How did she know all this? Had she been tuning in to Radio Jas?

I said, "Wow, how did you know all that?"

She was stuffing Libby into a pair of dungarees, so she had to speak quite loudly over the growling. I think Gordy was in the dungarees somewhere too.

"I'll tell you how I know, Georgia, because sadly, I know what rubbish your brain is full of. Get your coat on."

Charming.

Gordy is being left behind in a secure unit (Libby's old playpen with the table on top of it). Libby wouldn't let go of the bars of the cat prison until Mum let her pop Pantalitzer doll in with Gordy to keep him company.

I've never really got Pantalitzer doll. It has a weird plastic face with a horrible fixed smile, and the rest of it is a sort of cloth bag with hard plastic hands on each side like steel forks. It says "Made in Eastern Europe", so that is another place I won't be visiting.

Vati has gone off on what he calls a "secret mission"

with Uncle Eddie. He said to Mum, "I'll be back for you later. Keep yourself warm for me."

And then he snogged her. How disgusting is that?

Dr Clooney's

Oh, how very embarrassing all this is. I want to be home dreaming up my plan for entrancing Masimo. And also it's only seven days to the gig, and I haven't even started my cleansing and toning routine, let alone thought about making my eyes as sticky as possible. I should buy some more false eyelashes, otherwise known as boy entrancers. You can get some with tiny little sparkly bits in them. Or is that going a bit too far? I don't want to blind him, merely mesmerise him.

But maybe I have gone completely mad, like Ellen. Maybe I am just delirious with red-bottomosity. He only said it was nice to meet me. To be fair, he didn't say, "I want you to be my girlfriend." Or even, "Do you want to come out for a cup of coffee?"

Oh Lord. Perhaps I am just being *le grand* idiot.

Speaking of idiots, when we walked into Dr Clooney's waiting room, Mr Across the Road was sitting there. He's really cheered up since the kittykats were cruelly given away. He's especially cheerful that we have got Gordy. As he said, "Only a complete fool would take him in."

He said to Mum, "You're looking gorgeous as ever, Connie. Nothing wrong, I hope?"

Mum giggled in a horrible way. It's always like this when she's around men. Thank goodness I have a bit more dignitosity than her. I have certainly not learned my boy-entrancing skills from her. She said, "Oh no, I'm fine, thank you, we all are. It's just that Georgia is thinking of taking up a career in medicine, so we've come to talk to the doctor."

Mr Across the Road went, "Oh yeah, hahahahahaha... yeah, good one."

But then he realised that Mum was serious and crossed his legs. I don't know why.

Mum had her usual dithering attack when we went in to see Dr Clooney. He is very fit for a medical man. He said to me, "Any more elbow trouble, Georgia?"

"No."

"Lungs not making a peculiar wheezing noise?"

"No."

"So, what is it: eyebrows growing uncontrollably?"

I started to say, "Well, no, but if there's a cream that..."

But Mum was batting her eyelashes and speaking rubbish. "Well... hehehehhe, as you know, Georgia is very interested in science and medicine and so on... aren't you, Georgia?"

I said, "Well, I can do an impression of a lockjaw germ."

Mum glared at me, but Dr Clooney said, "Go on then."

And I did it.

Dr Clooney said, "That is very very lifelike."

I was quite flattered and said, "I can also do a hydra wafting plankton into its central vortex with its tentacles. Do you want to see it—"

But old Mrs Dancing-in-the-nuddy-pants-with-strange-men-and-calling-it-aerobics interrupted me. "So I was wondering, as she has to do work experience for school, if she could perhaps come into your surgery for the day."

Dr Clooney said, "Nothing would give me greater pleasure. I mean it. Nothing. The day that your family walked into my surgery, well... life hasn't been the same."

That's when we noticed that Libby had got a blood pressure bandage thing wrapped round her head like a turban.

In the clown car

I crouched down in the back of the Robinmobile as Mum rambled on. "He is so nice, isn't he? You know, so nice, isn't he?"

I didn't say anything, but that didn't stop her.

"He said nothing would give him more pleasure..."

I said, "I bet he's got a proper grown-up's car and not a clown car."

Mum got all defensive. "Your father loves this car, and it is not a clown car, it's quite stylish."

"Mum, if you had your face painted white with a red wig on and a clown nose, nobody would notice. They would think, 'Oh look, there's a clown driving a clown car,' and they would be right."

"Your dad has to have hobbies."

"Yes, but why do they have to be so crap?"

She started to tell me off, when a terrible thing happened: Uncle Eddie came round the corner. Not on his usual very embarrassing prewar motorbike and sidecar, but in another Robinmobile! Oh my God they were breeding. And Dad was sitting next to him. They both had goggles on.

They drove along beside us. When we got to traffic lights, they would draw up next to us and then "accelerate" away when the lights changed. Pretending to be a racing car. Libby loved it, but I just kept my head right down. Mum was trying to laugh it off, but I know she was thinking, "How did I end up married to him?"

Home

I had no idea that Pantalitzer was stuffed with pigeon feathers. It was like a pigeon snowstorm in the front room when we got back. Gordy's head was just poking out of a pile of feathers.

Mum went ballisticisimus. "This house is a bloody madhouse. He's worse than Angus!!"

Angus seemed quite pleased. Then Vati came bounding in and tried to grapple with Mum. She shoved him off and said, "Oh get off, Bob! First it's bluebottles in the garage from your fishing, now it's clown cars. I just want—"

"Him to be more normal?" I said helpfully.

Mum shouted, "NO!!"

"More absent?" I tried.

She turned round at the door and yelled, "I just want to

be more... more... ME!!!!"

Crikey.

10:00 p.m.

Anyone who's seen the size of my mutti's basoomas (which is practically everyone, as she is always revealing them) will not join in with her wish to be more.

Dad was going, "What did I do?"

But I have no time to sort out their lives. In fact, I wish they would shut up about themselves. On and on they go. They've had their chance, and now it's my turn.

My bedroom
Midnight

There has been a lot of murmuring and crying downstairs. It's keeping me awake. Then Dad started singing to Mum a song called "That's Why the Lady is a Tramp". Which personally wouldn't have cheered me up.

It's disgusting. They are snogging. My parents are snogging. I can hear the lip smackingness from up here. I'm going to soundproof my room.

12:10 a.m.

I wonder how I can casually bump into Masimo. He's bound to be surrounded by girls at the gig.

Hmmm.

Thursday April 21st

Got up early so that I can brush up on my boy skills from Mum's book.

8:10 a.m.

Good Lord. Apparently girls like boys to say stuff like, "You are the most beautiful girl in the world," and boys like you to go "Uummm" or "Oooohhhh".

Well, that is useful, because whenever I think about Masimo, my brain goes away on a short holiday to Idiotland, but even I should be able to manage "Uummm". Is that a high-pitched "Uuummm", or more of a "Uuermmmm", lower down?

You could alternate high and low, just in case.

Midday

Jas is still giving me her cold shoulders. Pathetico.

Miss Wilson had the nervy spaz to end all nervy spazzes

today in English. We were doing *MacUseless* and she had already told Rosie and Jools and Ellen off for doing "Let's go down the disco" during the witches' dance. Then Banquo (otherwise known as Moira Sanderson) said to the witches, "You should be women yet your beards forbid me to interpret that you are so."

And Rosie had a complete and utter laughing attack. It set all of us off. We had just about calmed down when Jas as Lady MacUseless said, "Thou creamfaced loon," and that set us all off again. I think I may have pulled something.

8:00 p.m.
Vati came crashing back from football with the "lads". I could hear them laughing and cracking open beer. I hope they don't come up to talk to me. Oh, too late.

8:05 p.m.
Vati and Uncle Eddie came trooping up, laughing like loons. I said, "I would love to chat, but I'm doing my English homework."

Vati went, "And you are studying *How to Make Anyone Fall in Love with You*, that well-known novel?"

Oh *merde*, I hadn't hidden the book. Now he will definitely be on my case for the next million years. I snatched it away, but fortunately before he could go on, the other lads yelled up the stairs. "Bob, come and look at this: Dave can get two legs down one trouser leg." And they went raving off.

I don't think much of the Portly One's fitness regime, supposed to convince Mum that he's a good catch. Uncle Eddie told me that Dad was sent off tonight at football after twenty minutes for persistently calling the referee, Mr Lancaster, "Maureen". Then he comes home and drinks beer.

If I have "little sense of responsibility", as Hawkeye says, I know who to thank for it.

8:30 p.m.
Mutti came home with Libby, and for a minute I thought I could hear Jas's voice. I hope Libby isn't doing impressions now. There was a knock on my door and it really was Jas's voice.

"Georgia, it's me. Can I... can I come in, please?"

Blimey. Jas was forgetting that she had eschewed me with a firm hand. I said in a dignity-at-all-times way, "Come."

And she came in all in a ditherspaz, with the piggy eyes

that are all too familiar a sight to me. She said, "Tom's going off for six months to Kiwi-a-gogo land."

I said, "*Non!*"

Then she started blubbing, "Six whole months! How can he go?? And leave me behind?"

I started to say, "Ah well, you see, when the Sex God said—"

But she blubbered on and on, "I mean, how can he just go? How?"

"Yes, well, that is exactly what happened when I was dumped for marsupials. I said—"

"I mean, I wouldn't go and leave him... I wouldn't." And she started the uncontrollable blubbing again. I shoved Charlie Horse in her arms and went downstairs for first aid.

When I went into the kitchen to get the milky coffee and Jammy Dodgers emergency rations, Libby was styling Gordy's fur into a sort of Elvis quiff with hair gel. Mutti was making her costume for the *Lord of the Rings* party. I wasn't aware that there was a prostitute in *The Lord of the Rings*, but as I have never got beyond the first mention of hobbits, I will never know. I said to her, "Dad got sent off for calling the referee 'Maureen' and you wonder why I got a bad report. By the way, please forbid Vati to wear green tights for this party, whatever happens."

She said, "Your father's got rather shapely legs."

Is she truly insane?

Then she said, "What's the matter with Jas? She just said it was something awful about Tom."

I said, "Hunky is going off to snog sheep in Kiwi-a-gogo land for six months."

Mutti said, "Oh dear."

And Libby went, "Oh dear oh dear oh deary dear deary dear dear."

I'd like to think she was being sympathetic, that's what I would like to think, but I'm not stupid enough.

I said, "I know what it feels like to be dumped for a wombat."

At that point Vati came in for another beer and a big hunk of cheese. He winked at us all. "Hi chicks."

And went out.

I looked at Mum. "I know what it's like to be dumped for a wombat, but I don't know what it's like to be married to one."

Mutti said, "Don't be cheeky. You could have worse dads, you know."

There was a bit of a silence then, broken only by the sound of farting from the front room.

The milk was boiling and I went to make Jas's emergency milky pops drink. Mum followed me and said, "So, what about Dave the Laugh?"

I went, "Huh."

And she said, "Isn't there anyone you like?"

I was a bit distracted, and before I could stop myself I said, "Well, the new singer for The Stiff Dylans is cool. He's called Masimo and he's half Italian and actually gorgey and fabby."

I immediately regretted having told her. In principle I think parents should really only be like sort of human purses, but I sometimes forget.

I needn't have worried that Mutti would be at all interested in me; she was rambling on about herself.

"I had an Italian boyfriend once. I met him in Rimini on a school trip. It used to take him an hour to get his hair right. I was on the beach with him one time and this girl in bikini bottoms and with high heels got on a motorbike and rode off."

Even I had to ask, "Do you mean she had only her bikini bottoms on?"

Mum nodded.

I went on, "Do you mean she let her nunga-nungas flow free and wild on a motorbike?"

Mum said, "Yes, and they weren't small."

I said, "Isn't it a traffic hazard?"

Mum said, "Well, that's what I said. I said to my boyfriend, 'Isn't that a traffic hazard?' And do you know what he said?"

I said, "No, what?"

And Mum said, "I haven't the slightest idea. He didn't speak any English."

And then she had a laughing spasm that Libby joined in with.

Is that what it's like in Spaghetti-a-gogo land?

8:45 p.m.
A little voice from upstairs went, "Georgia, I'm all alone up here."

My bedroom
Back in Heartbreak Headquarters, Jas and I snuggled up in bed and drank our milky coffee.

In between snuffling and slurping, Jas said, "How can I stop Tom going away?"

I could feel a touch of wisdomosity coming on.

"Well, Jas, there are of course two ways of looking at this."

"Are there? You mean the right way and the wrong way?"

"No, I mean your way and the trouser way."

She slurped attentively.

I went on, "His trousers want to go and see his brother and ferret around with vegetables. And you... er... don't want them to."

Jas said, "So are you saying... I should be more understanding when I say he can't go?"

I shook my head sadly. If I had had a beard, I would have twirled it. I went on, "No. What I mean, Jas, is that never the twain shall meet. If you try to stop him, he will have, you know, frustrated trousers."

"Frustrated trousers?"

"Yes, you know, his trousers want to go off on an adventure and you want them to hang around in your wardrobe of life."

"They might like it in my wardrobe."

"Ah yes, they might at first, but then they might hang in

your wardrobe for ages and then be too moth-eaten to wander free."

Jas said, "So you think I should let the trousers go, set the trousers free?"

"Yes, I think you should."

She looked thoughtful, which is a bit unusual and scary.

"OK, but Tom doesn't have to go as well, does he?"

Good Lord. I am on the brink of exhaustiosity. What is the point of me thinking up philosophical analogies if Jas thinks we really ARE talking about trousers?

Midnight

Poor Jasy Spazzy has gone home to her bed of pain. On one hand, I am really sorry for her, but on the other foot, I can't help remembering how she didn't give a flying fig's pants when Sex God went to Kiwi-a-gogo.

12:05 a.m.

However, to be a jolly good pal (and I sincerely hope that Baby Jesus is not having the night off in Africa or something and is therefore noticing my goodness, and planning a reward in the shape of a gorgey half-Italian half-Hamburger-a-gogo bloke). Anyway, what was I saying before I so rudely interrupted myself? Oh yes, to be a jolly good pal I may get her a Curly Wurly and wrap it up in special wrapping paper.

12:15 a.m.
Oh, I can't sleep. I wonder how I can get to Masimo and impress him with my whatsits. Feminine willies. If I wait until the gig, he will be quite literally covered in girls.

Dom told me he goes to St Budes art college. I could accidentally on purpose bump into him on my way home.

The fact that it's on the other side of town is a bit of a logistical problem. I may even have to bunk off school.

12:20 a.m.
Which might mean I would miss "gaseous interchange" in Blodge, which is a blow.

12:25 a.m.
However, as "gaseous interchange" is another term for breathing and farting, I can make up for lost time by being in the same room as my father.

"...and that's when it fell off in my hand."

Friday April 22nd
On the way to Stalag 14

Despite my very wise trouser speech to Jas, she has decided to punish Tom by not seeing him or speaking to him.

I said, "How long has this been going on?"

And she said, "Well, I didn't get home till quite late last night, so..."

"So... you haven't actually been able to ignore him yet?"

"No, but when I see him I will."

She is still very unstable and sniffly. I gave her my special Curly Wurly gift with its special Christmas gift wrapping. We were just walking up the hill when I handed it over. It didn't have a very good effect on Jas – she looked at it and then flung her arms around me and started really blubbing and wailing. She was saying, "Oh Gee, you are such a good pal and I've been horrid to you... I am sooooo sorry, I really love you. I know you are always asking me to say so and I never will, but I do. I do love you."

Crikey. She had gone bananas. I thought she would stop after a minute, but still she went on. I tried to walk on but I ended up sort of shuffling along with her hanging around my neck. I bet it looked like the lezzie version of *Blithering Heights*. All I needed now was for Masimo to come by. Or some notorious sadists like Wet Lindsay or Hawkeye. Then I thought of the worst-case scenario... Miss Stamp. If Miss Stamp came by now, she would be in Lesbian Heaven. She would ask us round to her place for "tea". She would offer me extra coaching... oh my giddy God...

I pushed Jas off me quite firmly and said sternly, "Jas, remember your Rambler's badge – don't let yourself down, remember the Country Code."

What on earth was I talking about?

It seemed to make some sort of sense to Jas, because she stopped sniffling and adjusted her beret.

I went on cheerily, "Six months isn't long... is it? It's only twenty-four weeks. You could do something really great in twenty-four weeks for when Tom comes back."

She said, "Could I... like what?"

I said, "Well... you could... grow your fringe out and that would be a good thing, wouldn't it? A new you, Jas, imagine it. A new fringeless you."

I could see I had got her attention, which is sad really.

Break

We have had an extraordinary meeting of the Ace Gang on the Blodge knickers toaster to discuss the Jastragedy. The nub and gist is that we have taken a sacred vow (you make the vow and then are given a Chinese burn by the person next to you). Anyway, the sacred vow that we will never break is: "We, the Ace Gang, will never let any boy come between us and the Ace Gang. We are all for one and one for all, once and for all." Or whatever it is that the Three Musketeers say.

I have to say in principle I agree, but in practice I crossed my fingers while I made the vow because, if I can snaffle Masimo, I'm afraid it is one for one.

English

I think everyone must have crossed their fingers, because our vow of sisterhood lasted about ten minutes. We'd just settled down for an hour of complete misery and bollocks (*Blithering Heights*) when two window cleaners bobbed up at the windows. They were not what you would call very fit-looking boys, but they were boys. And none of us had seen a boy for... er... about an hour and a half, if you don't count Elvis Attwood, which we don't.

The whole class had a massive dither attack. Some girls dived under their desks and started applying lip gloss and some started flcking their hair around like loons.

Miss Wilson said, "Now, girls, settle down, it's just a couple of window cleaners. You're all acting as if you've never seen a member—"

She was interrupted there by Rosie saying "Oo-er."

Miss Wilson went fantastically beetroot but carried on, "As if you have never seen a... a... person of the male... gender. Please show a bit of grown-up behaviour and don't let yourselves down." Then she started tripping lightly in the Valley of the Prehistoric. "When I was a young lady, I—"

Jools said, "Did you meet the Swan of Avon, Miss?"

Miss Wilson rambled on, "No, Julia, I did not meet the Swan of... er, it's not the Swan, it's the Bard of Avon."

Jools went on, "Oh so you knew him quite well then, if you knew his real name."

By this time most of the class were pressing themselves up against the windows and Miss Wilson had to go for reinforcements. Hawkeye soon saw the lads off into a different part of the school.

Boo. Still, at least it had passed a pleasant half an hour, and we hadn't been forced to wander round blasted heaths and so on.

Lunchtime

Practically the whole school has been tracking the window cleaners like they're pop stars, chasing them about and screaming. It's mad.

Wet Lindsay and her henchwomen no sooner hand out reprimands and beatings (not really, but they would obviously like to) than another group of girls creeps up.

Even the little first formers were prancing about, singing stupid songs like, "Window cleaners, window cleaners, give us a wave, give us a wave."

In the end Captain Mad (Elvis Attwood) set up a sort of armed guard to keep us at bay. Although, to be frank, I don't think a garden hoe is going to frighten some of the Upper Fifth if they decided to have a go. Melanie Griffith could just send her nunga-nungas on a lone expedition and he would be on his back.

Even Jas is cheered up, and she's determined to come to the gig to show Tom how much she's ignoring him. As I left her at her gate, she said, "You have got to help me ignore him and make him jealous and so on."

"Jas, I am not going to snog you for anything."

1:00 a.m.
I have got everything ready for tomorrow night, even though I want to play it cool and just sort of remind Masimo who I am. I am not going to be throwing myself at him or anything. I am going to play the callous sophisticate.

The callous sophisticate with really groovy false eyelashes, or my boy entrancers, as I call them.

Saturday April 23rd
It's like a hobbit house. Vati has got himself and Uncle Eddie big false ears. You can imagine how attractive Uncle Eddie looks in his. Also, I didn't know there was a gay elf in

The Hobbit but there is, and it's my dad. He's leaping around in his green tights going, "Oooohhh hello, I am Legalet!!"

Libby and Gordy have gone round to Grandad's for the night. God help them one and all; the mad meet the very very mad.

The most appalling thing has happened. The woman in the next-door madhouse to Grandad thinks she's his girlfriend and keeps knitting things for him.

Double sadly, she can't knit. As a lovely gift, she knitted him a jumper. It was only after ten minutes of him nearly suffocating that we discovered that she hadn't knitted a neck hole.

11:30 a.m.

I have got my bedroom to myself as make-up headquarters. Even Angus is out. He is defending his love for Naomi against her new suitor, Manky. If Mr Across the Road thought that Angus was Naomi's bit of rough he should see Manky, who is definitely her bit of rougher. Manky and Angus have already had a duel at dawn – Angus came home with a bit of Manky's tail as a victory souvenir. I may frame it.

4:00 p.m.

Now then, I've written a list of hit points for my plan:

1. Steam, cleanse and tone. Apply primer coat of pale ivory base, paying special attention to any lurker incidents.

2. Coat eyelashes with talcum powder for maximum build-up of mascara. (This is a top model tip – along with putting a white spot in the middle of your lips to make them look bigger – actually, I won't be doing this bit. I don't want any suggestion of Coco the Clown to mar my evening of LUUUUURVE.)

3. Dust all over face with powder to avoid the shiny twit look.

OK, I've done all that, now to point four.

4. Inspect for any orang-utan outbreak.

As I was trying to see the back of my legs in my hand mirror, Legalet came prancing in. "Hello, I'm Legalet and... Bloody hell, Georgia, what in the name of your grandad's outsize cycling shorts have you done with yourself – you look like a ghost!"

I leapt into my wardrobe and said from in there, "DAD, how DARE you look at me, I've only got my foundation coat on. And this is my bedroom. I don't come snooping around in your room. In fact, I have the good manners to ignore you."

As he went out, Legalet said, "Oh the joy of fatherhood, it never fades... By the way, what time do you want me to pick you up?"

What?????? He was dressed as an elf. An elf picking me up in a Robinmobile. Noooooooooo.

I said, "Hahahhhahah, er, don't you remember? Jas's dad is picking us up."

Fortunately he's too excited to question me closely about Jas's dad, who is in fact in Birmingham tonight.

7:00 p.m.

I don't ever remember being this jelloid before, not even when I had Terminal Horn syndrome for the Sex God. I can hardly move my eyelids for mascara and false eyelashes. I wonder if they look natural? I didn't get the ones with the false diamonds in them. I just got the thick long ones.

Oh I can't take them off now: it took me about a million years to put the glue on and stick them on. It isn't as easy as it sounds on the packet. What I go through for luuuurve.

Stiff Dylans gig

8:15 p.m.

We all got massive giggling gertie syndrome on the way to the gig. Even Jas joined in with the jollity; she is determined to let Tom know that she has a life of her own. I didn't point out the obvious fact that she hasn't, because I am full of sympatheticositisnosity. Which is not an easy thing to say.

Anyway, she's letting Tom know that he's not the only codpiece in the sea. Going along the High Street, clattering along on our high heels, we sang "The girls are back in town, the girls are back in town." We were doing the linking up thing. We all link arms and are not allowed to break the chain for any reason. It makes getting round corners or crossing roads practically impossible. God help any poor person coming the other way; they could be dragged along with us for hours. Strangely, people seemed to cross to the other side of the road when they saw us coming.

We were allowed to break armsies at the entrance to the Phoenix. I was soooo excited, and sort of frightened too. Ellen, Mabs, Rosie and Jas hadn't even seen Masimo yet.

In the tarting-up area (loos) we reapplied lip gloss for maximum snoggosity.

Rosie said, "What is your cunning plan, Georgia? Full frontal or glaciosity with just a hint of promise?"

I said, "Deffo glaciosity with a hint of p."

"Is that why you're wearing furry eyelashes?"

I gave her my special cross-eyed Klingon look. "These, Rosie, are not false eyelashes, they are boy entrancers. They hint at a sophisticosity beyond my years."

The Ace Gang went out into the club and I had one last check in the mirror. I practised my "sticky eye" technique. God, I was good – I practically got off with myself.

Out in the club it was really kicking, quite dark and groovy. In fact when I first came out of the tarting-up area, I couldn't see anything for a minute until my peepers got used to the lack of light. I don't think the boy entrancers helped.

The Ace Gang had formed a posse around Jas at a table near the front. Tom, the official ostracised leper, was at the bar with a couple of mates. I could see no one else of any interest apart from loads of lardy blokes and some girls from our school.

9:35 p.m.
My nerves are shot to pieces. I can't stand the tension of this. I have to go to the piddly-diddly department every five

minutes. Jas was making me worse. She was Ditherqueen and a half. Going on and on about Tom.

"Is Tom looking at me? Don't look."

"Jas, I can't see if I don't look. But don't worry, I'll be very casual. I'll startle you with my casualosity. I'll sip your drink and look through the bottom of the glass and see if he's looking."

I lifted up the glass and looked.

"He's not looking at the moment – oh yes, hang on, hang on... yes, he's looking now."

Jas said, "How does he look? Does he look upset?"

"Er. Hang on, there's a bit of ice cube in the way, I'll just eat it... er, he's talking to Matt... oh, oh now he's looking over here."

Jas said, "How is he looking? Is it just like looking looking, or is it like, you know, looking like he's made a big mistake wanting to go and snog sheep instead of staying with me?"

I said, "Jas, it's a bit difficult to tell looking through the bottom of a glass. Also, I'm getting neck spasm. Have I smeared my lip gloss?"

I am truly a bloody great pal.

10:00 p.m.

I hadn't even seen Masimo yet. I can hardly remember what he looks like. Maybe I had imagined he was groovy. I hadn't actually stood right next to him. Perhaps he was a bit of a shortarse, or maybe he had an irritating laugh. Or he'd grown a goatee. Or he liked elves... or—

Then the DJ said, "And now it's time for The... Stiff Dylans!!!"

And they came onstage. Everyone except Masimo. Dom said into his mike above the whooping and clapping, "Cheers, thanks a lot, we're back! And tonight we would like you to go wild for our new lead singer. He's not entirely an English person, but someone with a touch of Latin blood – calm down, girls – I give you... Masimo. *Ciao*, Masimo."

And Masimo came onstage. Oh crumbly knees *extraordinaire*. He is, as I may have mentioned before, the Cosmic Horn personified. The girls at the front were going bananas jumping up and down. (Which is not something I would try, even with my extra-firm nunga-nunga holders.)

I said to Jools, "How very little pridosity they've got."

Jools said, "I know, the next thing you know they'll be

creeping around backstage getting up on boxes and stalking him."

I said kindly, "Quiet now, Jools. I'm concentrating."

The hard thing to do is to be noticed but not to be noticed being noticed, if you know what I mean, and I think you do.

He was so gorgey and a fantasadosy singer and soooooo sexy. When he was singing you felt like he was really looking at you. He would have had a hard time, though, because I was practically under the table – I didn't want to reveal myself too soon... oo-er.

The joint was really rocking and we had to dance. It was like being at the sheepdog trials and dancing, because Jas was so paranoid about Tom getting to her we had to circle round her, dancing. When any one of us wanted to go to the piddly-diddly department, we all had to shuffle and dance off together and then shuffle and dance back to our place.

I was exhausted and managed to have a bit of a breather by the stairs, and it was there that Tom got me.

"Georgia, why were you looking at me through a glass for ages?"

"I... er... well..."

"Did Jas tell you to? Does she want to, you know, sort of

make up? I mean, it's only six months and it's such a great opportunity. Can't you make her see?"

"Tom, I have to tell you this: I'm Jas's friend and we are officially *ignorez-vous*ing you. You are a mirage to me, I can't even see you actually."

He said, "And nothing would make you help me?"

"*Non*, and also we have taken an oath involving torture."

He just looked at me.

"What if I could help you really casually bump into Masimo?"

"Pardon?"

"I met him the other night at snooker."

"You met him... he met you... you he..."

"Yes. And he'll come and say hello to me in the break and I could be casually talking to you."

I said with all the dignosity I could, given that my skirt was so tight, "And you think that I'd betray my bestest pal Jas just for some bloke I hardly know? When I've taken a solemn vow with Chinese burns and everything?"

Tom looked at me. "If you don't mind me saying so, you are quite literally criminally insane."

In the loos, Jas was sitting on the sink going on and on about her heartbreakosity. "He's a cad and a... user. He went out with me to fill in time until he could go and snog sheep."

Rosie, Ellen, Jools and Mabs were going, "Yeah, you're so right. Creep."

And, "Yeah, never have anything to do with him again."

Then they lost interest. Who wouldn't? And they all went back in to do mad dancing. It was just Jas and me. My little upset pally and me.

And only two minutes until the band had a break.

Jas was raving on and fiddling around with her fringe. I resisted slapping her hand because of her condition. Tempting, though.

She said, "I just can't believe him: all those weekends trailing badgers and mushroom hunting, I can't believe they just meant nothing to him. It's as if we never found that skylarks' nest..."

"Jas."

"Or that vole nest in the banks of the river..."

"Jas."

"I may as well never have learnt how to make a fire without matches."

I got hold of her.

"Jas, I think you should speak to him."

"What??"

"I think you should, you know, talk it over with him."

She stood in front of me, really red-faced. Bit scary actually.

"Georgia, are you saying that after all this, after all I've been through, I should TALK IT OVER with him?"

I said, "Er... yes."

And she said, "Oh, OK then."

She is unbelievably weedy, but I didn't say so because I wanted to check my boy entrancers before I went outside.

I said, "I'll go and talk to Tom first so that you don't lose your pridosity. I'll go and tell him that you might think about letting him explain himself. Then I'll come back to you, and you can look like you're shaking your head and so on and I'm trying to persuade you. Then eventually I'll tell him that he has four minutes and thirty seconds of your time. And I'll stand behind you with a watch."

11:07 p.m.

The band had left the stage by the time I went over to Tom. I said to him, "Mission accomplished. She will talk to you, but I have to go over and try to persuade her, but you'll know that we're acting."

Tom gave me a hug. As he was hugging me (and I have to say that even though I blame him for being the brother of a Sex God who left me for wombats, I do like him)... Anyway, as he was hugging me, Masimo came over from the dressing room. As he walked through the crowd it sort of parted before him. There was an awful lot of flicking of hair and smiling going on. And that was just the boys!!! No, really it was the girls, especially that trollopy Sharon Davies. She's had blonde streaks put in her hair. I don't think they look very natural. Not like my boy entrancers. I put an extra slurp of glue on them when I was in the loo just now, so there is no chance of them coming off. I was just watching Masimo. Not directly – I was looking over Tom's shoulder. As I was being Miss Cool I saw Wet Lindsay walk in with her sad mates. She had a ludicrously short skirt on. If I had legs as thin as hers I'd wear big inflatable trousers so that I didn't startle anyone. But she is too selfish to bother.

Ohmygiddygod, Masimo was coming our way. Tom winked at me. Then he called over to Masimo, "Hey, Masimo, *ciao.*"

Masimo heard him and smiled and came over. Oh please please don't let me go to the piddly-diddly department in the middle of the dance floor. When he reached us I could feel the heat of him being near me. Good grief and jelloid knickers akimbo. He said, "Hey, Tom, *ciao* – and it's you. Let me see... the lovely Ginger."

I went, "Hahahahahahahahahahaha" until Tom hit me on the back.

Tom said, "No, this is Georgia."

I said – even though I knew I should shut up, but you know when you should shut up but you go on and on, well I had that – "Ah well, you see, Libby thinks I'm half cat, half sister, and she... er... calls me Ginger sometimes."

Tom went on trying to rescue me. "Georgia went out with Robbie for a bit before he went to Whakatane."

Masimo looked me right in the eyes. "Robbie is, how you say in English... not in his right brains to leave you behind." And he smiled again. Phwoar! I had to look down because I couldn't trust myself not to leap on him.

I looked down and then I was intending to look up and do that looking up and looking away thing, and also possibly a bit of flicky hair. Unfortunately, when I tried to look up again, I couldn't because my boy entrancers had stuck to my bottom lashes. So my eyes stayed shut. They were glued together. I kept trying to open my eyes, but I couldn't. In sheer desperadoes I said, "Oh I love this one." And started wobbling my head around to the music.

The tune was Rolf Harris's "Two Little Boys", the naffest record known to humanity.

Ohmygiddygod, what should I do? I kept up the head waggling and I was raising my eyebrows up and down to pull my eyelashes apart. I bet that looked attractive. I thought I'd better do some humming. I started humming along to the tune.

Masimo said, "Would you like to have a drink?"

"Hummmmmmm hummmmmmm... No thanks, *non grazie*, I must groove to this one."

I must get away. I turned and head-wobbled off. I couldn't see a thing, obviously, so to stop myself from crashing into anything I put my hands out in front of me. But then I thought that would look odd so I tried to fit it into my dancing. I put one hand out in front and waved the other above my head like disco dancing. I knew the loos were sort of to my right and if I could just get there I could rip my boy entrancers off.

My "grooving" arm banged into something soft and someone said, "Oy, mind my basoomas, you cream-faced loon!"

It was Rosie, thank God. I said to her, "Rosie, lead me to the loos."

She said, "Clear off, you lezzie."

I was still madly flinging my arms around. Hopefully Masimo would think it was the eccentric English way of having a good time. Either that or he'd be phoning for the emergency services.

I said to Rosie, "My boy entrancers have stuck together. I can't open my eyes. Do something!"

She said, "Quick, put your hands on my shoulders and we'll conga dance over to the loos."

"Rosie, I don't think that's a very good—"

Before I knew it, she had forced my hands on to her shoulders and we were doing the conga.

Fifty-five million years later I broke free from the conga line – once we'd started doing it, the whole club had joined in. I yelled at Rosie to stop and take me to the loos, but she was having too much of a laugh. I got my hand to my eyes and tried to pry the lashes apart, and that's when it fell off in my hand – the boy entrancer I mean, not my eye.

I could see! I could see! I ran into the loos and ripped off the other one.

11:30 p.m.
I took a big breath and went into the club again. He had said I was lovely, and that Robbie had lost his brains to have left me. Which I think is a plus.

Tom and Jas were snuggled up in a corner talking and the rest of the so-called sheepdogs were all smooching with lads. That's when I saw Masimo. He was talking to Wet Lindsay; she had her stupid head really close to his.

In bed
1:00 a.m.
Raining.
Thundering.
Lightning.
Triple *merde*.
And a half.

1:05 a.m.

This is my unbelievable life: I am home in bed on Saturday. And my parents aren't even in yet.

How cruel is life?

If I had a Yorkshire accent and ate cow nipples, I would be an exact facsimile of Emily Brontë. I've probably contracted consumption by being out in the wind and rain.

Good.

1:30 a.m.

Ohhhh. What a crap night.

I didn't see Masimo again except on stage and he ignored me. I looked at him and I'm sure he saw me but he didn't smile or anything. Jas and Tom left early – so much for the strict four minutes and thirty seconds rule. At the end of the gig it was pouring down. Fabulous. Rosie, Jools, Ellen and I hovered about near the door waiting for the rain to ease off a bit. For once in my entire life I would have been glad to see Legalet drive up in the Robinmobile.

In fact, as an Ace Gang, we were quite literally hoisted by our own petards (which can be quite painful). Every single one of us had said that someone else's dad was definitely going to pick us up.

In the end we made a mad dash for a big tree across from the Phoenix, and we were planning what our next shelter would be when we saw Dom and the rest of the band come out and load up the van. It was raining so hard it was splashing up from the ground. Masimo wasn't anywhere around.

Then Wet Lindsay came out in her stupid leather coat with a stupid umbrella. All by herself, even deserted by her saddo mates. Teehee. I said to the gang, "Oh how thrice pathetico! She has to wait for her vati!!! Hahahaha."

Ellen said, "Still, she hasn't got two gallons of water down her neck like I have."

I said, "Look, she's all shuffly. I bet her thong is killing her. I hope so."

I was just thinking that we could button our coats together and make a sort of tent over our heads when I heard a scooter revving up. And Masimo appeared on his cool scooter with his parka on. I had a heart lurch. Then he pulled up to say good night to the rest of the lads. And then – and I can hardly bring myself to think about this – Wet

Lindsay got on the back of his scooter. I thought he'd kind of shove her off, but he didn't. He took her umbrella and held it over her while she put on a spare helmet, then he tucked the umbrella away and they motored off.

Rosie said, "Bugger me."

I got absolutely soaked on the way home but I didn't even notice. I was wet inside.

1:40 a.m.

Mutti and Vati are back, going "ShhhhhSSSSSSHHHHH" really loudly. They've brought Libby and Gordy with them.

1:45 a.m.

At last they are quiet and have gone into their bedroom.

1:48 a.m.

Vati has just farted "God save our gracious queen" and Mutti and he are apoplectic with laughter. Mutti stopped for a bit and then Vati said, "Now for verse two." And they started laughing again.

They are sad.

But at least they have each other. I haven't even got

my little sister in bed with me. I have no one who loves me.

And I never will have.

I really like him.

Once more in my bed of pain, crying.

2:01 a.m.

I think I must have cried myself to sleep, because the next thing I knew I had a big soggy cat bottom in my face. I opened my eyes to find four eyes staring back at me. Well, three eyes looking at me actually, and one was looking at the wardrobe. Angus and Gordy were absolutely soaking. They were doing shivering and cat sneezing. I said, "Go away into your baskets AT ONCE!"

Angus rolled over and started rubbing himself dry on my duvet. At first Gordy attacked Angus, in between sneezing, and then he started wiggling and diving into my duvet and burrowing under it near me. Urgh! I fished him out and lifted him up until we were eyeballs to eyeball and said, "Gordon, you are a very very bad kittykat – go into your kittykat basket!"

And he did that halfwit cat thing; he just let the tip of his tongue loll out of his mouth and left it there. Looking at me with the tip of his tongue sticking out.

Why do they do that?

Once they had both got nice and dry, they started scampering and crashing around in the dark in my room.

I put my head under the pillow.

Sunday April 24th

I went for a long moody walk across the fields. I didn't want to be in to answer questions about last night. I didn't even want to talk to my mates.

That is really it for me now, I've endured too much heartbreakosity for one lifetime. I'm going to concentrate on getting good exam results and then maybe going off to the Congo (wherever that is) as a doctor to help sick people. Even though sick people get on my nerves. I am at Dr Clooney's on Tuesday, so I may pick up a few hints about not letting moaning minnies get on my nerves. Surely there are no Mr Next Doors in the Congo?

I am sooooo depressed.

4:30 p.m.

About eighty messages from Jas. I suppose I should phone her.

5:00 p.m.

"Jas, it's me."

"Hi, Georgia. Tom told me how weird you were with Masimo. I thought you really rated him."

"I do."

"Well, why did you just go off waggling your head to a Rolf Harris song?"

Before I could explain, she started her famous rambling.

"Tom and I have come to an agreement. We're going to swap rings. When Tom goes off to Kiwi-a-gogo, our rings will mean that we'll stay true to each other until he comes back."

I didn't have the energy to stop her raving on.

"Also, as he says, it's a great opportunity to collect loads of data and stuff that he can bring back and that we could, you know... look at."

Old Rambley Knickers is back then. I think I preferred her when she was all upset and clinging round my neck.

Still, at least someone's happy.

I said to her, "You know, after you left, Masimo took Wet Lindsay home on his scooter."

Even Jas paid attention then.

"*Non.*"

"*Oui.*"

"Georgia, that is *très très merde*. Why did he do that?"

"I really don't know. Boys are a bloody mystery to me."

Jas said, "Shall I ask Tom to find out? He's a boy."

"I don't know, Jas, I don't want any more pain and—"

"Well, if I just casually ask him and don't make a big deal about it."

"Well, I suppose if it was a little secret—"

Then I heard her going, "TOM!! TOM!! GEORGIA WANTS TO KNOW WHY MASIMO WENT OFF WITH WET LINDSAY LAST NIGHT."

I couldn't believe this was happening. I tried to get her to shut up. Then I heard her mum shouting from somewhere, "Jas? I thought you said that Georgia liked Masimo. Why's he gone off with Lindsay?"

Jas said, "I don't know. That's why I asked Tom."

Jas's mum shouted, "What do you think, Tom?"

When Jas's dad joined in the conversation I put the phone down.

9:30 p.m.

Ring on the doorbell. Oh now what? Everyone is at Grandad's. It might be kitty trouble because I don't know where the furry psychopath twins are (Angus and Gordy).

I could just ignore the bell. No one would know anyone was in.

Except all the lights are on.

Oh God, if it's the cat vigilante group bringing the lads home on an assault charge, I'll go ballisticisimus, if I have the energy.

It can't be anything to do with the furry hooligans, because they're in the lavatory drinking out of the lavatory bowl. Erlack.

Opened the door in my jimmyjams, which I put on for comfort. They're a bit like Jas's knickers – on the large and shapeless front – but who cares, nobody is going to see me in them.

Crikey!!! Dave the Laugh. He leant against the door. "Hi gorgeous. Blimey, HUGE pyjamas!"

I went into the goldfish routine. "I... well... I..."

He said, "Can I come in? I bring you tidings of great joy, and it's not even Christmas."

I said, "Er, well... come in and er put the kettle on..."

"Do you think it'll suit me?"

I dashed upstairs when Dave went into the kitchen and did a rapid lip gloss, blusher, mascara fandango, and pulled on my jeans and a T-shirt. No time for nunga-nunga holders, I would just have to move very slowly with my arms crossed. *Pant pant.* I went into the kitchen.

Dave was wrestling with Gordy on the kitchen floor, and when he stood up Gordy was attached to his sleeve and just dangled there like a tiny ginger loon, which he is.

"Speaking as your Horn adviser, I've come to tell you I've just seen Masimo."

I went even more lurgified. Gordy crashed to the floor.

I managed to stutter, "Did, he say... was he, did he, was I... you know."

"I still say he's flash, but anyway, what in the name of arse made you walk off on Saturday? He thought you were very up yourself."

I said, "My boy entrancers got stuck together and then one fell off."

Dave said, "Your boy entrancers stuck together and then one fell off?!" And he was looking at my nungas to see if I still had two.

I said, "No, no, I mean my false eyelashes. First of all, I looked down and they got glued together and I was blind. So I sort of shuffled off to the music to try and unglue them, and then one fell off, so I had to go to the tarts' wardrobe."

Dave said, "Tarts' wardrobe?"

"Loos."

Dave said with sort of admirationosity in his voice, "Outstanding!"

Midnight

As my official Horn adviser, Dave says I must be friendly and smiley but play hard to get and not give up if I really like Masimo. Dave also said that because Masimo is so flash and Italian, even if he does quite rate me – despite the Rolf Harris fiasco – that will not stop him falling for flattery from other girls. Even Wet Lindsay. Dave also said that Masimo doesn't know anyone in town or any history, so he wouldn't know that Lindsay was wet and a worm and a thong wearer.

12:10 a.m.

Anyone would know that Lindsay was wet and a worm; just look at her legs for God's sake.

Anyway, if he falls for old knobbly knees, why should I want him? Mind you, the ex-Sex God went out with her for a bit. Hmmm.

Dave says that boys fall for that useless obvious stuff because they have boy insecuriosity – different from girl insecuriosity. It's because they are knob-centered, allegedly. Although I think that Dave just likes to talk dirty.

1:00 a.m.

Dave says you can't drop hints with boys because they don't get it.

1:10 a.m.

In my *How to Make Any Twit Fall in Love with You* it says:

1. You can never flatter boys too much; they will never know you are being ironic.
2. Never use hints with boys, because they don't get it. You have to ask for what you want.

It is vair vair tiring, this boy bananas.

2:00 a.m.

Also why does my Horn adviser always snog me?

2:05 a.m.

More to the point, why do I always snog him?

I suppose in the land of Cosmic Horn everything is fair.

Monday April 25th
German

Tried out my flattery technique on the dithering champion for the German nation. Herr Kamyer was wearing a pair of tartan socks, clearly visible beneath his shin-length leisure slacks. He was telling us about his riveting childhood in the Bavarian Alps. His childhood mostly consisted of camping and clapping games, interspersed with two tons of sausages. And the *Volk* of Lederhosen land wonder why they have a reputation for total crapness.

At the end of the lesson I went up to Herr Kamyer as he was packing up his books. I startled him a bit by coming up quietly behind him, and there was a minor ditherspaz incident. As he was picking his books up from the floor, I said, "That was really *sehr* interestink, Herr Kamyer, and may I compliment you on your attractive socks."

To my absolute amazement, he said, "Ach, thank you very much, Georgia. Der socks are from my mother and are a personal favourite of mine. I also have a matching tie."

I said, "Oh, I'd love to see that."

Herr Kamyer adjusted his glasses. "Vell, I vill vear it to show you."

I said, "That would be marv."

He went off all smiley and twitchy. Surely it can't be this easy. It must be because I've chosen quite literally a soft option.

Break, Knicker Toaster Headquarters

I told Rosie and Jools my news and the advice from Horn Headquarters (Dave the Laugh).

Rosie said, "I believe Dave, but Herr Kamyer's not really a bloke, is he? He's a German teacher. I bet you can't make it work on Elvis."

Lunchtime

The ultimate test. Elvis Attwood, the grumpiest bonkerist man in the universe.

Rosie and Jools insisted on being witnesses to what they

said would be an abysmal failure. They hid behind the science block loos.

Elvis was as usual prodding around (oo-er) pretending to do gardening. It is, as we all know, just a perving tactic so that he can try and see girls in their sports knickers. He should become a gym mistress, he easily could. If he grew his hair and wore a gym skirt, he would be Miss Stamp's double.

I approached Elvis casually.

"Afternoon, Mr Attwood. I'm sorry to hear that you will be leaving us." I could hear Rosie practically exploding behind the loos.

Mr Attwood looked up with that incredibly attractive grimace he keeps especially for me. I gave him a beaming smile, letting my nostrils flow free and wild for once.

He said, "What do you want? Have you been messing around in the science block? I found a drawing that was supposed to be me on the blackboard."

I said, "Oh, that's nice."

He said, "No it's not bloody nice, it was disgusting."

I said, "Was it the one of you in the nuddy-pants with an enormous pipe?"

He said, "Yes, that's it."

I said, "No, I haven't seen that one."

He grumbled on, "It's a scandal the way you lot carry on. Call yourselves young ladies? In my day you would've had your ears boxed."

I said, "Well, I agree with you, Mr Attwood. I think discipline has gone right out of the window. I mentioned it to Miss Heaton in detention but she wasn't interested. Do you know that in the Isle of Man they still beat people with twigs if they do wrong?"

He drew himself up to his full height (two and a half feet). "Yes, well, it would make you think twice if you got some twigs across your derrière instead of all this talking."

I said, "Yes, I do so agree talking is crap, Mr Attwood, 'scuse my language. I've often said in RE I would rather be beaten by twigs, but you can't tell people, can you?"

Mr Attwood looked a bit puzzled at the turn of events.

I said, "I don't know if you know this, but us girls all sort of look to you for a firm lead, Mr Attwood. I know you think we mess about, but actually we have a deep respect for you. You're a sort of father figure and naturally we rebel a bit, but at the end of the day we respect you."

You could see Mr Attwood squaring his shoulders. "When I was a lad we were given a decent set of rules. I was in bed by eight thirty and up by six thirty to do my chores."

I said, "Actually, my parents are much the same with me: early to bed, early to rise and so on."

There was a crash from behind the loos, as if someone had fallen over.

I said, "Well, thank you very much for your time, Mr Attwood. It's very good to have someone who's like a father figure."

Mr Attwood lit his pipe. "Well... yes, well, anytime. Do you know you've made me go back a bit to when we had simple pleasures: for instance, I've got a train set I had as a lad, in perfect condition, still in its box—"

"Gosh is that the bell? I must get along to English, we're doing *Blithering Heights*."

When I got behind the loos Rosie had her coat buttoned over her head to stop her laughing.

On the way home
4:15 p.m.
Lolloping along with Jas, I said, "It can't be this easy. It just can't be."

Jas said, "I know, it just can't be."

Four boys from Foxwood came by doing their usual orang-utan walk and shouting rubbish at us.

"Come on, girls, get them out for the lads."

I said to the one with terminal acne, "Hey, you're really nice-looking, would you like to see my nunga-nungas?"

He stopped doing his orang-utan impression. They all stopped.

He said, "Er... yes."

And I said, "Well, I wouldn't just for anyone, but, well, I've noticed you before... Meet me by the park loos at seven thirty."

And he straightened his tie and said, "Oh yeah, I think I can make that."

Unbelievable.

Absolutely unbloodybelievable!

Me and Jas just looked at each other.

Tuesday April 26th

Today is my work experience day at Dr Clooney's, so up at the crack of nine.

Quite groovy to put on make-up and ordinary clothes on a school day.

Mmmm, I wonder what's suitable wear for a doctor's surgery.

Black?

Yes, I think so.

Boy entrancers?

Oh yes, I think so. Even though there will most definitely be no boys to entrance, apart from Dr Gorgeous. It means I can get my staying-on technique right in the safety of the Valley of the Unwell.

5:10 p.m.

Good grief. Said goodbye to Dr Gorgeous. God bless him and all who sail in him, but I will never, ever, be returning to his surgery except on a stretcher and unconscious. It's hell on wheels in there.

Just a load of sick people moaning and sneezing. If I haven't got scarlet fever or Old Person's Lurgy, I'll be amazed.

Moaning and moaning on for hours. How can Dr Gorgeous stand it? And such a terrible pingy pongoes smell. It's the old men, mostly. I wonder if they get mixed up with their aftershave and mothball liquid. Or Bovril.

Perhaps there's a perfume called "Old Bloke" that's a big hit with the elderly and sends all the older ladies wild, knitting neckless jumpers and so on.

Anyway, that's it, there's a career I will never be having. I will not be going to the Congo. Which is just as well, as I haven't been able to find it on the map.

5:40 p.m.
Oh I was soooo happy to be alive and free. Free, free. I felt like scampering and skipping down the road. Plus my boy entrancers had stayed on all day with no suggestion of glue-eye.

I was singing a song in my head and moving my hips in time to the music. Like it said in the book. A car honked its horn as it went by and some boys shouted out to me. Probably moron boys, but it's a start. Now, if I could just add the flicky hair I would be laughing.

So let's see... hip, hip, flickyflick, hip, hip, flickyflick. Excellent!!! Now for the *pièce de* whatsit – downy eyes and upsy eyes.

Hip, hip, flickyflick, uppy, downy, hip, hip.

Yesssssss!!!! Got it. I am a Sex Kitty.

Once more, with feeling.

Hip, hip, flickyflick, upsy, downsy eyes—

"*Ciao.*"

Ohgreatballsof*ordure*: Masimo!!!! On his scooter. Saying *ciao*.

I looked up. Yes, there he was.

I said, "Oh, *ciao.*"

How cool was that? Very very cool. Cooler than that, it was vair vair vair... shut up brain, shut up!

Masimo was still looking at me, like he thought that at any time I would start closing my eyes and dance off. I said, "How are you?"

Excellent. Normal as Norman Normal. Normaler.

He looked at me with his fab eyes. It would have been weird if he'd looked at me with anything else, with his ears for instance. Hahahahahahahaha. Oh God, I was doing out of control laughing in my head!!! This was a new and scary development on the nincompoop scale.

Masimo said, "I am cool."

I thought, *You can say that again, mister.*

Masimo revved up his engine. "Can I give you a lift anywhere?"

Blimey.

"I am going to rehearsal. Maybe I could drop you at your home."

Oh yes, that would be groovy, him dropping me at my house and seeing the Robinmobile, and maybe my mum in her aerobics outfit... or Libby in no outfit...

I said, "Well, I'm going to my mate's house. We're hanging out before we go clubbing."

What am I talking about??? Clubbing? I will be going clubbing – clubbing myself to death if I keep talking absolute arse-blithering rubbish. Then Masimo smiled at me and I got chocolate body syndrome, which is jelloid knickers with knobs. He gave me his spare helmet – great news, I would have pancake hair when I got to Jas's and took it off. But I didn't really care.

I climbed on the back of the seat. It felt really groovy, but I would have to think of a good way to get off that didn't involve a knickers extravaganza. I wasn't exactly dressed for bike work as I had my very very short black kilt on. Maybe if I shuffled over and put one foot on the floor and then bent the other knee up and sort of slid... Masimo said, "Hold on to me." And accelerated off quite fast. I put my hands on his waist. He had his parka on and everything, but it was like I got an electric shock touching him. The wind was blowing in my face and making my eyes water. Please don't let my boy entrancers blow off.

We sped along. It was really fab and I was feeling full of happiosity and bliss. I couldn't believe I was actually on the back of a scooter holding on to the Sex Meister.

Masimo shouted to me, "Please, tell me how to get to your friend's house."

Actually, Jas's house was about five minutes away, but I directed Masimo to go down the High Street even though that wasn't on the way. When we stopped at the lights I saw Dave the Laugh's Rachel and a few of the Upper Sixth going to Luigi's. They all waved like mad when they saw Masimo, even Rachel... Masimo just raised a gloved hand and we whirled off. I hope everyone recognised me under my helmet.

I could have stayed holding on to Masimo and riding round for ever: round and round, like that bloke on that doomed phantom boat, *The Flying Dutchman*. Of course, there are differences – he was not on a scooter, and I don't have a beard and am not Dutch.

Eventually I had to point out Jas's house to Masimo and

we pulled up outside. I got off without a police incident but Masimo didn't turn his engine off. I didn't think that was a good sign. It meant he wasn't going to hang around and chat.

I tried to remember some Italian and said, "Well thanks, er *gracias* a lot. Thank you a lottio. Thank youio a lottio."

Masimo smiled. "I am glad for doing of it. I am, how you say... full of sorrows for my English."

I said, "Oh don't worry, I hardly speakio any myselfio."

He laughed and said, "You are funny."

Oh brilliant, he thinks I'm funny. Not groovy or a Sex Kitty that he must spend the rest of his life worshipping and adoring, but funny.

Then he said, "I must go to my rehearsal."

And he revved up. I said, "Oh yeah, well *ciao*." Then I remembered my Horn teacher's advice so I put on my biggest smile. "It's really nice that you've come to town and... I... thought you sang *très bon*."

He smiled again. "Good. Thank you. I will see you. *Ciao*."

And he went off. I turned to go into Jas's gate feeling a bit flat and in the Valley of the Terminally Confused again. Had he just given me a lift out of politeness? Oh damn, damn and damnity damn damn. I hate all this.

I looked at him as he reached the end of Jas's street. He could be going to see Wet Lindsay after rehearsals for all I knew. How did she get boys to like her...? It was a bloody mystery. Maybe she slipped horse tranquiliser into their Coke?

As I was watching him indicating right, he did a big wheelie and curved back up the street very fast towards me. He slowed down in front of me and shouted, "Georgia, do you want to come with me to the cinema?"

I did my world-famous impression of a cod in a kilt. He turned the bike round again and said, "If you do, I will see you at seven thirty on Friday at the clock tower. *Ciao, va bene.*"

Then he sped off.

I rang on Jas's bell and eventually she answered it.

"Have you come to test me on my Froggy assignment?"

Is she really truly mad? I said, "Jas, be sensible. Let me in and give me something."

"Like what?"

"Sugar. I've had a shock. Get your secret chocolate stash out and I'll tell you."

As we were munching away in her bedroom, I told her all about it.

She said, "Blimey. So he's actually sort of asked you out."

"I know, fab isn't it?"

"But is he seeing Wet Lindsay as well? Maybe it's a double date thing and she'll come to the cinema as well, and you'll have one of those French things."

"What French things?"

"You know, *ménage à trois*."

"Jas, he's Italian."

"Oh well, menagio à trios."

8:00 p.m.

I had to leave because sometimes Jas is so sensationally mad that I feel violence coming on.

But nothing can alter this fact: Masimo, the best-looking bloke in the universe, a Dream God, has asked me – Georgia Nicolson – to go out to the cinema with him.

8:30 p.m.

I might have known there would be a couple of flies in the ointment, one of them quite porky. Mutti and Vati were in a real strop and a half when I got in. Vati started, "Where have you been? And before you start, don't give me any nonsense about homework club. I wasn't born yesterday, you know."

I felt like saying, "Not unless yesterday was eighty-five years ago."

But I didn't because I love everyone.

Then Mutti joined in. "You have got be straight with us, Georgia. If you want to be treated like a grown-up, then you have to show us you deserve to be."

Vati was still grumbling on, "It's not like we've never been young, but I at least treated my parents with respect and told them the truth."

I said to him, "Are you suggesting you want me to tell you the truth at all times?"

Mutti said, "Of course, my darling, we're your parents."

I said reasonably, just to clear things up, "Ah yes, but when I said how crap the Robinmobile was and why did we have to have a clown car, Vati went ballisticisimus."

They both just looked at me in that sighing, looking-at-me way. Still, I was in Cloud Nine land and maybe I would make a point of telling the truth from now on.

I took a deep breath and said, "OK then, I'll tell you. I was walking home from Dr Clooney's after a hard day with the elderly mad when the new singer from The Stiff Dylans came along and gave me a lift to Jas's on his scooter."

Vati was already a bit huffy. "How old is this 'lead singer'?"

I said patiently, "He's Italian."

Vati said, "What?"

I said, "He's Italian, isn't he, Mum?"

Vati looked at Mum. "So you know all about this then, Connie? What is it with you two? I'm always the last to know anything in this house. I slave away all day and then when I come back..."

I slipped out while he was raving on and went to my room. It doesn't matter what happens – divorce, orphanosity – it doesn't mean anything when you have a Sex Meister as your plaything.

9:00 p.m.

Libby has made Gordy a pair of cardboard glasses at nursery school. And a hat to hold them on.

Actually it's not a hat, it's a rubber glove, but it holds them on nicely.

11:00 p.m.

I haven't got long to plan my outfit for Friday.

Should I try to get Mum to buy me something new? Knowing her, she'll probably count the new kitten-heeled boots and two skirts and trousers she bought me on Saturday as new.

I wonder if I should consult with Dave the Laugh before I go on my date? No, because I don't want any chance of rogue snogging.

I'm so excited I am never going to go to sleep again.

Zzzzzzzzzzzzzz.

Wednesday April 27th
Breakfast

Vati gave me a squeeze on the shoulder as I was eating my Frosties. And he and Mum seemed to be speaking. What fresh hell?

He said, "Georgia, thank you for telling us the truth Here's a fiver to get yourself something. Remember, it's always worth telling the truth to people."

I said, "Oh, well, if fivers are involved, I should tell you that I'm going to the cinema with Masimo on Friday night."

I thought Vati might explode, but sadly he didn't. He tried

♡ 233

to go on being reasonable, which was scary to witness He was mumbling as he got his flying helmet on, "Right. Good. Right. That's the sort of thing we mean. Good, right."

And then he went off to Flood Headquarters.

Honesty is definitely going to be my policy from now on.

Break, on the knickers toaster

I had been going through with the Ace Gang what I could wear on my date. And also showing them a new celebration dance I'd made up for the occasion. There was, I must admit, quite a lot of finger pointing and hip waggling in it, but that's the way with celebration dances.

Rosie said, "Georgia, you know that you're one of my bestest pals and that the Ace Gang is all for one and all the way to Tipperary and so on."

I said, "*Oui.*"

"However, if you go on being such a prat and a fool for much longer, I'm afraid I'm going to have to kill you."

Games

The Upper Sixth were getting changed when we came into the changing rooms. We are being forced to do a cross-country run by Adolfa. But I don't mind because it means I will be in tip-top physical condition for my love date on Friday. (Of course, it will also mean that tonight I will be in bed by five thirty with severe exhaustion and bottom strain, but *c'est la vie*.)

Then I saw Wet Lindsay eyeing me like a Seeing Eye dog and also talking to her astonishingly dim and limp mates about me. I wonder if she knows anything about me and Masimo. Why should she? Still, it gives me the creeps. I feel that we have shared past lives together, and they have all been crap.

Detention
4:20 p.m.
Oh God and *Gott in Himmel* and also *Mon Dieu*. What is the matter with Hawkeye? She is so unreasonably surly. I went to the loos before Latin and I was just sort of dollydaydreaming about Masimo, so I was a tiny bit late for class. Herr Oberführer Grupmeister of the Universe (Hawkeye) said, "You should have been here at three p.m."

And I in a fit of spontaneous combustion and honestosity said, "Why, did something really good happen?"

I have to write out eight hundred times, "Rudeness is a poor substitute for wit."

Which is quite literally a pain in the arse. I mean it. I can hardly sit down after our cross-country run. At least I can walk, which is more than can be said for Nauseating P. Green. She should never have attempted the water jump in her condition (i.e. very fat).

4:25 p.m.
Hurrah, I have perfected a way of doing lines quickly. I've Sellotaped five pens to a ruler so I can do five lines at once.

The fifth line looks like a mad woman's knitting, but you can't have everything.

Thursday evening, April 28th
Jas is staying behind after school. Hard to believe that a human being can be interested in going around the sports field with the Blodge teacher looking for vole droppings, but that's old Jazzy Knickers for you. The most interesting person since... er... Quasimodo.

I must say, though, I am relatively impressed *vis-à-vis* her glaciosity and independentology towards Tom. I think he's definitely very puzzled about how calm she's being, and he's not talking so keenly about going any more.

once more into the oven of love

Friday April 29th
Lunchtime

Time is going so slowly.

I said to RoRo, "Do you think I should risk the boy entrancers?"

She said, in between mouthfuls of cold rice pudding, "What if there's a snogging incident? I mean, you know, they might get entangled in something."

"Like what?"

"His moustache."

"He hasn't got a moustache."

"I know, but if he had one. I'm just saying you can't be too careful."

Please don't let me emigrate to Madland just before the best evening of my life.

I don't think I will risk the boy entrancers, though.

4:30 p.m.

I ran home with gay nunga-nunga abandon. I ran and ran with a devil-take-the-hindmost attitude and hoped I wouldn't see anyone I knew. Thank the Lord for once that I didn't. I can only imagine what I looked like.

5:35 p.m.

Bathed and moisturised to within an inch of my life. Face pack on.

Should I make a list of conversational topics so that I don't accidentally say anything abnormal?

6:00 p.m.

The trouble is, I don't have anything normal to say. I can't talk about my family life when my vati has a clown car and my mutti has no moral code. I can't even begin to go into Libby, or Angus and Gordy. Or Grandad.

What about school and my mates?

Am I mad????

Hmm, well, what about books I've read?

Surely no one really wants to know about *Blithering Heights*, and somehow I don't think I should mention

How to Make Any Twit Fall in Love with You.

So that leaves make-up.

Oh God.

7:15 p.m.

I'm taking tiny tiny steps so that I am not early or hot. I honestly don't think I'm going to be able to speak: my throat feels like something has nested in it. Maybe I should just not turn up. He's bound not to like me. He probably won't turn up. He's Italian and fab beyond marvydom and older. He's got girls hurling themselves at him. I should just stick to my own league. That's what it says in my book. I just read it before I came out. It says you should choose someone in your own sort of area physically. If you are an eight you can choose a seven or another eight. But how do you know what you are? When Jas, Rosie, Jools, Ellen and I did that points out of ten for features, I got a nine for my hair but minus zero for my nose. Does that mean I'm an average seven? Because if it does, I'm definitely buggered because Masimo is beyond a shadow of a doubt a ten.

7:40 p.m.

I'm going to go home. He's not going to come anyway, and I can't hide in this shop doorway for much longer pretending to be looking at kitchen implements.

7:42 p.m.

Oh blimey, here he comes now. He's just ridden up on his scooter. Right. Casualosity at all times is called for.

Masimo had his back to me, so fortunately he didn't see me nearly fall over when I didn't see the wheelchair ramp thing on the pavement. He was locking up his scooter and then he turned to look around. God he is gorgey. He had a cool blue and grey Italian zip top on and a suit. Honestly, I don't think I've ever seen any of my boy mates in a suit. It looked really groovy gravy. But it did make him look like a grown-up. Still, I was being a grown-up myself(ish). He saw me and looked at me for what seemed like ages. I felt like doing some Irish dancing to fill in the time, but I didn't.

Then he sat down on the seat of his scooter and watched me come across to him. He said, "*Ciao*, Georgia, you look very gorgeous. Forgive me for being late."

Hell's biscuits, I don't think I can stand this. I managed to croak out those immortal and sophisticated words, "Oh hello."

He left his bike on the pavement at the clock tower, which I don't think is altogether legal.

We walked along to the Odeon. He was walking along quite close to but not touching me, although when we got to the door he opened it for me and sort of put his hand gently in the small of my back to guide me through. He only had to brush against me for my entire insides to start doing morris dancing. He paid for our tickets and we went into the dark and sat at the back in the official snogging seats. That must mean something, mustn't it? Or didn't he know they were the snogging seats? Oh dear *Gott in Himmel*. I kept thinking I must say something interesting, but what would be safe?

Before the film started, Masimo got us Cokes and he said, "So, Miss Georgia, you are quiet."

I said, "Oh yes, well, I'm just relaxing because it's been mad lately."

Masimo said, "Oh yes, what have you been up to?"

"Yes, well, I had to... er... do a cross-country run and—"

Fortunately he interrupted me. He said, "So do you like

sport? I am big sport fan. I like the football and I run, every day I run."

I said, "Oh yes, so do I. Nothing stops me running. If the weather is too bad I run around my room."

He laughed for quite a long time. So I laughed as well. But actually I do run around my room, and who can blame me?

We watched the film, but I can't remember a thing about it because of the extreme tensionosity. My shoulder was right next to his, and when he gave me some popcorn his hand brushed across mine. It gave me such heebie-jeebies that I nearly had a spasm and chucked the popcorn everywhere. I definitely was on the road to Spazzyville.

8:45 p.m.
Halfway through the film and still no sign of snogging. He's brushed my hand, our shoulders and knees occasionally touch, and that is it. Perhaps he found he didn't fancy me when he saw me and now he's just sitting politely through the film.

Perhaps he never even thought of me in that way.

Maybe I am like a chum.

Oh GOD.

We went out into the night and Masimo said, "I will give you a lift home."

No suggestion of coffee or anything. So he definitely thinks I'm a mate. I am so depressed. But I cannot be a sad sack. I have to pretend to be perky and that I like being a mate to a Sex Meister who I just want to leap on and snog to within an inch of his life.

The Sex Meister seemed to know everyone we saw. He'd only been here for a week or two and all the girls in town seemed to know who he was. It was all "Oh *ciao*, Masimo," fluttery, fluttery, flickyflick. Pathetic.

I said with a really nice smile, "You seem to have got to know a lot of people."

He said, "Yes, they are nice. I don't know... the girls, they are very friendly here."

Hmmm, "friendly" was one word for it. He seemed to be a bit sad somehow. As we got near the clock tower, he said, "It's nice, it's just that, well, in Italy I had a girl, you know, a serious thing and it ended. She was sad, I was sad. So now I, how do you say... I have burned my hands in the fire of love."

One minute it's Dave the Laugh the Horn Master telling

me it's all to do with the Cosmic Horn and hormones, and then the Sex Meister goes all poetic and burns his hands on the oven of love.

Masimo smiled at me. "So now, I don't want to be sad any more. I want to be happy, have fun. Do you want to have fun, Georgia?"

I said, "Er... oh yes, Fun City is where I live usually. I'm a bit like you, really. When Robbie went off to Kiwi-a-gogo I moved from Love City to Fun City. Obviously stopping off in Sad City."

He laughed. "I understand. I think. So this is good, it is all fun."

"Oh yes, absobloodylutely fun as two short... fun things."

We got back to his scooter and got on it. He helped me into my helmet and as he fastened it he looked straight in my eyes and said, "Ah *caro*... you are sweet."

Then he hopped on and revved up and we scooted away. I loved being on the back holding on to him as we whizzed through the dark streets. It was like being in an exciting movie, except I didn't know whether it was a romance or a comedy.

We got to my house and I got off the scooter sharpish in

case of knicker display, took off my helmet and juujed my hair. He switched off the engine. Ahahhahahaha. Then he said, "Georgia, what do you know of Lindsay? Is she one of your mates?"

Er, what exactly was the correct answer to that? I would rather eat my own poo than be her mate, she's a slimy twit with the smallest forehead known to humanity. Or just a simple "I hate her to hell and back"? But then I remembered that I was "funny and sweet", not "a massive bitch", so I said, "Er... Lindsay, well, yeah, she's, you know... well, yeah..."

And left it at that.

Masimo said, "She has got for me a ticket to 'Late and Live', which would be groovy to go to, do you think?"

I smiled and nodded. I hope the smile came out right because as my mouth was smiling, my brain was going "Kill her, kill her, strangle her with her thong, stick her in a bucket of whelks..." Now I knew what it felt like to be Angus.

Then I saw Vati peering through the curtains. Oh God, now he was waving in a cheery casual way. He went away, and then Mum appeared waving and smiling. Stopwavingandsmiling!!! The only plus was that the Robinmobile was in the garage. Sadly, Angus and Gordy weren't. Gordon is not even officially supposed to be out at night. He's still wearing the glasses Libby made for him, although they are now on sideways. Angus and Gordy were wrestling with each other on the wall. I said, just for something to say, "That's Angus and Gordy."

Masimo went over to the wall; he was smiling. "Hey, they are great."

When Masimo got near, Angus stopped wrestling and sat up staring straight at him. Oh God, I hoped he hadn't got anything against Italians. Gordon came and sat next to him and they were both staring at Masimo. Then they both did the letting the tips of their tongues loll out of their mouths. Like idiot cats.

Why did they do that??

I couldn't think of a single normal or even "fun" thing to say after all the shocks I had had, so I said, "Well, I suppose I should go in now, it's a bit nippy noodles. Thank you for a fab night."

And Masimo said, "Ah yes, *ciao*." And he got on his scooter and started it up. Then he looked at me and kicked the scooter back up on its stand but left it running. He climbed off and came over to me. "Yes, thank you, Georgia."

And he put his face near mine and I thought, "Yes, yes, and thrice yes, he is going to snog me. At last, at last!!!"

And then he did kiss me. But just a tiny baby kiss. It was over in a second and really gentle, like brushing my lips with his. No suggestion of tongues or any handsies. Just a sort of peck.

And that was it.

He said, "See you later."

And roared off into the night.

Midnight

I am exhausted. What in the name of Sir Richard Attenborough's baby-doll nightie was all that about?

Saturday April 30th
10:00 a.m.

I can't believe this. Two more of Vati's sad mates have bought Robin Reliants. There's a clown car convention in our driveway. Vati and his incredibly sad mates are standing around discussing wheels or their new red noses or something. I'm hiding in my bedroom until they all go. They're all off to a rally, thank the Lord, which means at least I can be on my own with my miserablosity.

10:30 a.m.

Mutti came up to say goodbye and give me a kiss, even though I buried my head under my pillow. She said, "I am kissing the pillow where your head is and you can't stop me."

I went, "Hmmmfff."

She said, "We'll be back about eight. Eat something sensible, and that doesn't mean a jam and chip sandwich. By the way, that Italian boy is quite literally gorgeous."

Oh oh!!! Nooo, she was talking about him. No no. Shutupshutup.

11:00 a.m.

Peeking out of my curtained window as the Clown Rally departs.

I really can see why the youth of today are so ashamed of the older generation. You should see what Mum and Dad are wearing. They are all in leather. Vati has a leather jacket and trousers on, as well as his flying helmet and goggles, and Mutti has a leather minisuit on and thigh-length leather boots. She looks like a prostitute. And Dad looks like a brothel madam.

Libby, Angus and Gordon all have their own flying goggles now. There was a lot of late-night fighting, but in

♥

the end Libby persuaded Mum and Dad that Angus and Gordy had to go to the rally and needed goggles.

So there they are, sitting in the back window of the Robinmobile with their gogs on. Don't ask me why Libby wields such power over them. Angus is supposed to be my furry pal. It was quite nice last night having him purring away on my nungas when I was so upset. I thought he would hang about with me today to keep me company. Especially as I got up so early to feed him – I was out in the garden in the freezing cold at eight thirty.

I have a method for giving him his food that prevents any accidents (like me having my hand gnawed off). The method is, I lock him out of the kitchen and then I put his pussycat snacks in his kittykat dish (Gordon has his own eatery in the downstairs loo – it's handy because then he can have a thirst-quenching drink from the lavatory bowl... erlack). Anyway, I put Angus's food in his dish whilst he amuses himself by hurling himself at the door, like a furry battering ram. Then I let myself out through the kitchen door into the garden, and go to the front door and into the hall where Angus is headbutting the kitchen door. Protecting myself with the broom, I open the door and he dives in. Then I shut the kitchen door. So I'm never at any time in the same room as Angus and food. That's why I have two hands.

But this means nothing to him. One word from Libby and he's got his goggles on and is in the back of the Robinmobile. I'm surprised that he's not driving. He will be on the way back.

12:00 p.m.
Phoned Jasyissimus, my bestest pal.

"Jas?"

"Oh hello. What happened then? What number did you get to?"

"Oh, Jas, I am so full of confusiosity."

I told her what had happened. She sounded as if she was thinking – you could quite literally hear the cogs in her brain going round. Then she said, "So what you are saying is that officially you didn't even get on the snogging scale with Masimo."

"Well... no, we didn't... I mean, he handed me my Coke and touched my hand."

"But he didn't hold it?"

"No."

"Well, it's not number one then, is it? Unless you've added 'handing over a Coke' to the snogging scale without telling me. And what number would 'handing over a Coke' be, anyway? You might as well have a number for 'saying hello' or..."

She was beginning to annoy me quite badly. She's the opposite of telepathic – she's tele-pathetic, because she just goes on and on no matter how much she should just shut up. On and on she rambled...

"So, he didn't put his arm around you, so that's nil points so far. What kind of good-night kiss was it?"

"Well, you know, he put his lips on mine and—"

"For how long?"

"Er... about er two seconds."

"Two seconds??"

"Yes."

"Two seconds??"

"Yes yes, how many more times?"

"He put his lips on yours for two seconds?"

"YES, JAS!!"

"Well, that's not a kiss, is it? My aunties do that."

Then I finally snapped. "Well, that is because you have lezzie aunties – my aunties don't put their lips on mine."

"I have not got lezzie aunties!!"

It deteriorated after that and we both did stereo phone banging down.

1:00 p.m.

I tried to eat but it's no use, my tummy's all knotted up.

Jas is right, actually. I got nil points on the snogging scale because Masimo didn't want to snog me.

He wants to snog Wet Lindsay, but not me.

What's so wrong with me?

2:30 p.m.

Looked in the mirror.

There is the spready-nose thing. Could that be it? But Robbie and Dave the Laugh didn't seem to mind it.

My eyes are OK. I got mostly eights for them.

And my hair's OK. It's a bit of a boring brown, but since the snapping-off incident I haven't wanted to mess about too much.

My eyebrows are more or less under control.

Oh, I don't know.

Perhaps it's my nose. Someone did give me zero for it.

And that was its highest mark.

3:30 p.m.

Phone rang. It was Rosie.

"Gee, why haven't you rung me with all the goss?"

"Because there isn't any. Masimo gave me a sort of peck on the lips and said I was sweet and that he was going to 'Late and Live' with Lindsay."

Rosie went quiet and then she said, "OK, my little pally, I think we need to call an extraordinary meeting of the Ace Gang. Be round at my house at four p.m. for snacks."

I love Rosie.

But not in a Jas's auntie way.

4:10 p.m.

Rosie had made jam sandwiches with the crusts cut off as a special invalid dish for me.

She said, "Everything's going to be all right. I've got oven chips for later."

God, I think I'm becoming a lezzie. It would be a damn

sight easier than living in Heartbreak Hotel all the time.

Jools, Ellen and Mabs arrived, and Jools said, "To open our official Ace Gang meeting and as a tribute to Billy Shakespeare, Miss Wilson's boyfriend, I say, 'Let us indeed goeth downeth the disco!!'"

And we did our special disco inferno routine. Which I did have to say cheered me up.

We were all lolling and panting on the sofa when the doorbell rang.

Rosie came back in with Jas. We looked at each other and she said, "I am preparing myself to forgive you."

Which is tosh and a facsimile of a sham, as it is her who is in the wrong. It's not my fault she has lesbian aunties. But I didn't say that because frankly I need all the friend support I can get.

I told them my Masimo story and they all nodded wisely and fed me jam sandwiches.

At the end I said, "So what do you think?"

Rosie looked very very wise and owly and said, "Well, after hearing everything... this is what I think: number one, he's Italian."

We all nodded.

"Number two, he's a boy."

We all nodded again. It was like a nodding-dog convention. Rosie was just looking at me, nodding her head. I said after about twenty-five years of nodding, "Yes, and so?"

She said, "So... frankly, I haven't got a clue what it means."

The rest of them all went, "No, me neither..."

Qu'est-ce que c'est le point????

Sunday May 1st

I am going quite literally bonkers. I hardly slept last night. Masimo was going to go to "Late and Live" with Lindsay, so from about seven p.m. that was all I could think about.

How could he like her?

I suppose she is older than me.

But so is Slim, our revered headmistress, and Masimo doesn't fancy her.

I don't think.

Although anything could happen in a life full of people with no foreheads and lesbian aunties.

Now I really feel sick. I've just had an image of Slim in a short skirt with her massive elephantine legs jellying around on the back of Masimo's scooter going off to some gig.

9:30 a.m.

Not that it would drive off if she were on the back of it.

In fact, if she sat on the back of it, Masimo would probably shoot up into the air. Which would be a good thing.

9:40 a.m.

No it wouldn't. I really like him. It's not his fault he wants to have fun after a serious relationship. I cannot point the finger of shame at anyone with the General Horn. I too have heard the call of the Horn.

10:00 a.m.

But I really do like him.

It's just not fair that he doesn't like me.

1:00 p.m.

I've got big bags under my eyes. And I think I might have lost weight. I've only had jam sandwiches and oven chips for the last twenty-four hours. And cornies and toast that Mum brought me this morning, but that's all.

2:00 p.m.

All alone again, the Mad have gone to Grandad's. Yesterday was the Clown Convention and now today is the Mad Convention.

Angus, Gordy and Naomi are all in their bachelor pad, the Prat Poodles' kennel. Mr and Mrs Next Door have gone out and left the Prat Poodles to the mercy of the kittykats. Angus, Gordy and Naomi have finished the nice doggie dinner they found in the kennel and are now having an after-lunch game of Chuck the Squeaking Bone About. It's driving the Prat Poodles insane but they daren't come out from behind the dustbins.

3:00 p.m.

I've tried everything to take my mind off Masimo – played really loud music, yoga, chanting, praying to Baby Jesus, plucking my eyebrows. In the end I was so sheer desperadoes I even did my German homework.

4:00 p.m.

Rang Dave the Laugh. He answered the phone.

"Dave, it's me, Georgia."

"Aha, hello, Sex Kitty, just couldn't help yourself then. I know what you mean. I may have to get bodyguards soon, I'm so gorgeous. Sometimes I want to snog myself."

"Dave, I... want... well..."

Oh God I was going to blub.

He said, "What is it?"

I said, "I'm really really upset."

He sounded serious. "Are you, pet? Why? Tell me, or shall I come round?"

I said, "Well, I suppose you're... well... busy."

"Do you mean am I with Rachel? You know what I told you about boys, Georgia, you have to spell it out, you can't be subtle."

"Yes, OK, are you with Rachel?"

"No, I'm not, we went to 'Late and Live' and it was a late one, so she's with her family... Anyway, whatever, shall I come over?"

5:00 p.m.

Dave and I walked over the back fields, even though it was extremely nippy noodles. I told him what had happened. He said, "Yeah, I saw Lindsay and Masimo last night. He's incredibly flash, Georgia, he had a suit on – although I must say I didn't see his handbag."

I knew I should have been expecting it, but I still just wanted to blub. Dave put his arm around me. "Listen, I'll tell you the truth from a Horn Master's point of view. I think Masimo is playing the field. He can have anyone he wants so he's bound to be tempted. You said that he had a serious thing in Italy – and he wants to get over that and have fun. But I do think he likes you, because, well, despite being certifiably insane you are a lovely, funny Sex Kitty. And actually you are quite a sweet person."

I couldn't help it, I gave him a really big hug and tears came out of my eyes. Dave got out his hankie and dabbed them away. Thank God I'd thought better of wearing my boy entrancers. Who knows what would have happened when Dave dabbed my eyes. I could have ended up with a false moustache.

10:00 p.m.
Dave's advice is to not give up and be cheerful, but to be realistic. He says I should believe in myself and think I am the bees knees and then other people (boys) and maybe even Masimo will think I am too.

I don't know why, but I sort of believe him.

260

He's actually a great mate.

And Horn advisor.

He's a proper boy mate.

Who's like a mate.

And not a boyfriend.

It's relaxing just to talk to a boy and not have snogging on the menu of life.

Midnight
So how come we got to number six??

Tuesday May 3rd
Pelting down.

I said to Jas as we trudged along under our umbies, "My heartbreak has given me a new dignitosity."

Jas said, "Is that why you're walking funny?"

I gave her my special biffing on the arm that makes your arm go paralysed. It was her umbie-holding arm and she nearly speared a couple of first formers walking in front of us. That perked them up.

Assembly

Uh-oh, it's the fainting season again. We usually have an outbreak just before exams. Kathy Smith and Rosemary Duvall keeled over during "All Things Bright and Beautiful" and had to be carried out. Lucky swine. Slim said, "Settle, girls, settle, they will be quite all right."

Just then Isabella King crashed to the ground. They were falling like flies. I might try it myself: we've got double Physics next. Unfortunately Hawkeye was on the warpath. I could see her giving Isabella the third degree.

Slim was still aquiver. "You must all make sure you have a good breakfast; not eating causes fainting."

I said out of the side of my mouth, "No danger of her keeling over then. Do you reckon she stores extra supplies in her chins?"

Rosie started uncontrollable laughing. I can feel hysteria coming on.

As we left the hall, Wet Lindsay was beaking about. I looked at her and she had a really smug look on her face. She is so thin and useless, what can Masimo see in her?

Physics

We liberated the anatomy skeleton from the Blodge lab and put "Fatty", as we call him, in science overalls. We sat him at the back in between me and Rosie. Herr Kamyer is so duff that he didn't even notice until the skeleton put his hand up to answer a question.

Lunchtime

Ace Gang meeting in the science block lavs. I told them what my Horn advisor had said – well, I didn't actually say that Dave had told me, I let them think it was my own wisdomosity – and they all started nodding.

I said, "Please don't start the nodding fiasco again."

Jools said, "So what's your plan? Are you going to kill Lindsay?"

I said, "No, that would be childish. And I am displaying maturiosity these days. So I'm not going to kill her; we are all going to start a staring campaign."

The plan is that we all stare at a part of Lindsay every time we see her. Like her nose. Or her lack of forehead. Or her stick legs. And so on. She will get paranoid that she has a bogey hanging out of her nose, or her skirt is tucked in her knickers and so on.

The second part of my mistress plan is to get in tip-top physical condition by going running every day. Then when I'm fit as a frog I will casually find out where Masimo goes running and turn up. Like a fabulous running Sex Kitty. And he will be bowled over by my charms, although hopefully not by my nunga-nungas.

I will wear my new sports bra to keep them under control.

Simple pimple.

3:00 p.m.
Excellent progress in the staring campaign. I gazed at Lindsay's chin when she was talking to her stupid tragic pals in the corridor. She got all shuffly and then I noticed she went off to the loos. Obviously thinks that she's got a lurker. Hahahahaha. *Excellente!!*

3:45 p.m.
Jools, Ellen and Jas all gazed at the top of her head and they said she went off to the loos again.

She'll be practically living in there by the time we've finished.

4:30 p.m

Rightio. Part two of my luuuurve plan. Running begins.

4:32 p.m.

It has stopped raining but Gordon Bennet it's nippy noodles, I can see my breath freezing. What kind of stupid weather is this for May? No chance of nip nip emergence, though, because I have got my nungas safely strapped in.

5:00 p.m.

Phew, I'm boiling and out of breath. I thought I would be quite fit after hockey and everything but I'm not.

5:10 p.m.

I might not be able to breathe but at least I'm not being knocked out by my basoomas.

5:15 p.m.

Right, I'm going to just cut across the top of the field and then come down the hill and go home.

Can heads explode? Because I think mine is going to.

There is some other fool out running. I can hear pounding along behind me but I haven't got the strength to look round. When I get home I'm going to get in the fridge, I'm so hot and red.

"*Ciao*, Georgia."

Ohmygiddygodspyjamas, Masimo!!!

Nooooooooooooooooooooooo.

He caught up with me and was running alongside me. I just kept running and turned and gave him what I hoped was an attractive smile. Attractive if you like a smiling tomato in a jogging outfit. He looked sooo cool, and not even sweating. Also he seemed to be able to breathe. And talk.

He said, "You know, I didn't get your phone number. Would it be possible that you tell me?"

I gave him another smile. It might be the last living thing I did. Then I saw the hill path and my brain was so starved of oxygen it had no control over any part of my body. My legs started stumbling down the hill path. They were just merrily careering down the path, carrying my head and body along with them. Thank God Masimo didn't follow me. As he continued along the top path he shouted, "OK, Miss Hard to Get, I will see you later when I get back from America, *ciao caro*."

At that point the hill path curved round and I crashed into a bush and fell over.

In bed
9:30 p.m.

Oh ow ow. Ouch and ow.

He wanted my telephone number and I couldn't speak. I could only be very very red.

I can't stand this.

I hobbled downstairs and phoned Dave the Laugh.

"Dave, he asked me for my phone number tonight but I couldn't give it to him because I was too red. He called me 'Miss Hard to Get'."

Dave said, "Excellent work. You are of course studying at the feet of the Horn Master."

11:00 p.m.

Boys truly are weird. Dave says that I have accidentally done the right thing, I have become the mystery woman.

11:10 p.m.

He said, "See you later when I get back from America."

That's far beyond the usual "see you later" fandango.

Wednesday May 4th

Evening

Today was fifty million hours long. I have made Jas find out from Tom who can find out from Dom what is going on with Masimo.

8:30 p.m.

Jas said, "Masimo has gone to London for a week and then he's off to Hamburger-a-gogo to visit his olds."

11:00 p.m.

Hamburger-a-gogo land.

11:10 p.m.

Merde.

11:15 p.m.

Vati roared up in the Robinmobile. Bang bang clatter clatter. Shout shout. He is so shouty and trousery.

Then Mutti started going, "Wow!! Oh Wow. Fantastic!"

Pray God he's not got some new even more embarrassing trousers.

Oh dear *Gott in Himmel* and Donner and Blitzen, now they're tramping up the stairs to my room. They burst in and I pulled the blanket over my head.

Mutti said, "Go on, tell her the news. Tell her!"

Now what?

Vati said, "We're off to America at half term!"

I shot up in bed.

Midnight

I hugged my own father.

12:05 p.m.

We are off to Hamburger-a-gogo land. I can track down Masimo.

12:10 p.m.

I don't know exactly where he is, but how big can America be??

P.P.P.S.

Look, I don't want to go on and on about dim people because it is unnecessary and rude. And also they won't understand.

However, in the interest of World Peace and harmonosity, I have written a glossary (and please don't tell me that you don't know what a glossary is, because that would be taking quite literally the piss).

I love you all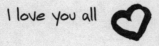

Georgia's Glossary

airing cupboard · This is a cupboard over the top of the hot-water heater in a house. It is used for keeping towels and sheets warm on cold winter nights. Er, at least that's what it's used for in normal people's homes. In my home it is Libby's play den or Angus and Gordy's winter headquarters. It is therefore far from hygienic. In fact, you would be a fool to put anything in there.

arvie · Afternoon. From the Latin "arvo". Possibly. As in the famous Latin invitation: "Lettus meetus this arvo."

BacoFoil · Aluminium foil for cooking things in the oven. By the way, did you know that Hamburger-a-gogo types leave out the second "i" in aluminium. If they can't be arsed to have vowels later on in words, where would we be? Do they say plutonum? Or titanum? No, they don't. Otherwise the whole thing would just become a sham and very very tedus. Not to menton confusng.

Blimey O'Reilly · (As in "Blimey O'Reilly's trousers".) This is an Irish expression of disbelief and shock. Maybe Blimey O'Reilly was a famous Irish bloke who had extravagantly big trousers; we may never know the truth. The fact is, whoever he is, what you need to know is that: a) it's Irish and b) it is Irish. I rest my case.

Blodge · Biology. Like Geoggers – Geography, or Froggie – French.

BluTack · Blue plasticine stuff that you stick stuff to other stuff with. It is very useful for sticking stuff to other stuff. Tiptop sticking stuff actually. I don't know why it's called BluTack when it clearly should be called Blue Sticking Stuff. Also, blue is spelt wrong, but that's life for you.

Bovril · A disgusting drink that is supposed to be good for you. It's made out of cows' feet. It is. Well, I think it is.

boy entrancers · False eyelashes. Boys are ALWAYS entranced when you wear them. This is a FACT... unless of course they get stuck together and then boys think you are mad and blind and not entrancing at all.

clud · This is short for cloud. Lots of really long boring poems and so on can be made much snappier by abbreviating words. So Wordsworth's poem called *Daffodils* (or "Daffs") has the immortal line, "I wandered lonely as a clud." Ditto, Rom and Jul. Or Ham. Or Merc of Ven.

Curly Wurly · A choccy woccy doodah bar that is all curly and whirly. See milky pops.

div · Short for "dithering prat", i.e. Jas.

do · A "do" is any sort of occasion. A celebration. Say it was your birthday, I would say, "It's your birthday, let's have a bit of a do." Or, as in Elvis Atwood's case, I would say, "Let's not have a leaving do, can't he just go?" Or perhaps I'm being a bit harsh. No, I am not.

dodie · Dummy or pacifier.

duffing up · Duffing up is the female equivalent of beating up. It's not so violent and usually involves a lot of pushing with the occasional pinch.

Ethelred the Unready · Ah, I am glad that you asked me this because once more I am able to display my huge talent for historiosity. Most English kings and queens get nicknames like "Richard the Lionheart" (because he was brave and so on) or "Good Queen Bess". Ethelred (who lived a long long time ago, even before Slim was a young boy) is famous for being "unready". The Vikings came to

England to pillage and shake their big red legs at the English folk. They sneaked into his castle and caught Ethelred in the loo, and took over the castle. Hence his name – Ethelred the Unready. He's lucky that is all he's called. Things could be much worse: he could be called Ethelred the Pooey, or Ethelred on the Looey.

fives court · This is a typical Stalag 14 idea. It's minus forty-five degrees outside, so what should we do to entertain the schoolgirls? Let them stay inside in the cozy warmth and read? No. Let's build a concrete wall outside with a red line at waist height, and let's make them go and hit a hard ball at the red line with their little freezing hands. What larks!

fringe · Goofy short bit of hair that comes down to your eyebrows. Someone told me that American-type people call them "bangs", but this is so ridiculously strange that it's not worth thinking about. Some people can look very stylish with a fringe (me) while others look goofy (Jas). The Beatles started it apparently. One of them had a German girlfriend who cut their hair with a pudding bowl, and the rest is history.

gorgey · Gorgeous. Like fabby (fabulous) and marvy (marvellous).

half-term · Oh, of course you must all know what this is, you are toying with my emotions, you naughty minxes. A term is when you have to go to school, i.e. spring term, summer term, autumn term, etc. Half-term is halfway through the term when you get time off the sentence for good behaviour. Not really – you get time off because otherwise all the teachers would have a nervy b.

heavy manners · This is Jamaican patois and means keeping you under surveillance and possibly house arrest. I had a Jamaican mate and instead of saying "hi", or "hello", he would say "iry". But I thought he was saying "highway", so I would say "highway" back. He thought I was obsessed with motorways. It can be very difficult to get on with other nations if they will insist on speaking their own languages.

hobbit · Do we really have to do this? Oh God, are we never to be free? A hobbit is one of those little creatures in *The Lord of the Rings* with really big ears. They're bloody lucky to get away with just the ears compared to a lot of the other horrible things in the books – orks and so on. Is there anyone in *The Lord of the Rings* who is normal? Answer: no. The whole thing is a nightmare of beards.

japes · Enid Blyton wrote children's books about the Famous Five in the 1950s. These five complete wets and weeds had lots of "japes" and "jolly wheezes". If, for instance, they hid behind the door and then leapt out to surprise their parents, that would be a "wizard jape".

I think you get the picture of what extraordinarily crap books they were.

Kiwi-a-gogo land · New Zealand. "-a-gogo land" can be used to liven up the otherwise really boring names of other countries. America, for instance, is Hamburger-a-gogo land. Mexico is Mariachi-a-gogo land and France is Frogs'-legs-a-gogo land.

Late and Live · A late-night gig that has live bands on.

loo · Lavatory. In America (land of the free and criminally insane) they say "rest room", which is funny, as I never feel like having a rest when I go to the lavatory.

lurgified · This is an extension of the word "lurgy". To have the lurgy is to either have a physical or mental illness; so you could have the flu, but you could also have "stupid brain", which is what happens when you see a gorgey bloke and become "lurgified" – touched by the lurgy.

milky pops · A soothing hot milk drink for when you are a little person. (No, not an elf, I mean a child.) Anyway, what was I saying? Oh yes, when you are a child people give words endings to make them more cozy. Chocolate is therefore obviously choccy woccy doo dah. Blanket is blankin. Tooth is tushy peg. Easy is easy peasy lemon squeezy. If grown-ups ever talk like this, do not hesitate to kill them.

nervy spaz · Nervous spasm. Nearly the same as a nervy b. (nervous breakdown) or an F.T. (funny turn), only more spectacular on the physical side.

nippy noodles · Instead of saying, "Good heavens, it's quite cold this morning," you say, "Cor – nippy noodles!!" English is an exciting and growing language. It is. Believe me. Just leave it at that. Accept it.

nub · The heart of the matter. You can also say gist and thrust. This is from the name for the centre of a wheel where the spokes come out. Or do I mean hub? Who cares. I feel a dance coming on.

nunga-nungas · Basoomas. Girls' breasty business. Ellen's brother calls them nunga-nungas because he says that if you get hold of a girl's breast and pull it out and then let it go, it goes *nunga-nunga-nunga*. As I have said many, many times with great wisdomosity, there is something really wrong with boys.

Pantalitzer · A terrifying Czech-made doll that sadistic parents (my vati) buy for their children, presumably to teach them early on about the horror of life. I don't know if I have mentioned this before, but I am not sure that Eastern Europeans really know how to have a laugh.

parky · Another jaunty word for nippy noodles.

pash · Passion. As in, "I had a real pash on him until I saw his collection of vole droppings." Or, in Masimo's case, "He is my one and only super-duper pash." That is official.

pingy pongoes · A very bad smell. Usually to do with farting.

polo neck · I am not pointing the finger of shame anywhere, but did you know that in Hamburger-a-gogo land they call polo necks "turtle necks". Having a neck like a turtle has never been a big selling point for me... but let them have it their own way if the Hamburgese LUUURVE turtles so much.

rate · To fancy someone.

Robin Reliant · Oh, please, please don't ask me about this. Oh very well. You know how old blokes keep inventing things? For no reason? Well, they do. There's always some complete twit from a village called Little Beddingham or Middle Wallop – anyway, somewhere where there are no shops or television (or a decent lunatic asylum), and the complete twit is called Nigel or Terence and he invents things like a tiny shower for sparrows, an ostrich-egg cup, or a nose picker. You get the idea. Anyway, one of these types called Robin invented a car that only has three wheels. A three-wheeled car. Er – that's it. That was his brilliant invention. No reason for it. It's a bit like that bloke who invented the unicycle. All they do is encourage clowns. They should be stopped really, but I am vair vair tired.

scheissenhausen · Quite literally (if you happen to be a Lederhosen-type person) a house that you poo in (*scheiss* is poo and *haus* is house). Poo house. Lavatory. Or rest room as Hamburger-a-gogo types say. No one knows why they say that. Oh no, hang on, I think I do know. When they all lived in the Wild West in wooden shacks, one

room was both their bedroom and their lavatory. Cowboys
didn't mind that sort of thing. In fact they loved it. But I
don't.

Sellotape · As you know, this is usually used for
sticking bits of paper to other bits of paper. But it can be
used for sticking hair down to make it flat. (Once I used it
for sticking Jas's mouth shut when she had hiccups. I
thought it might cure them. It didn't, but it was quite
funny anyway.)

Sherpa Tensing · When English people were
stopped from conquering places by spoilsports who
said, "Clear off, this is our land," we had to have Plan B.
Plan B was to conquer other things, like mountains.
English blokes began hurling themselves up Everest like
knobbly-kneed lemmings. The Everest folk got sick of
them falling off or wandering around saying, "Where
am I?" and blundering into their villages day and night

in unnecessary anoraks. So they (the local folk – called Sherpas) decided to lead them up Everest just to get rid of them. And the head Sherpa-type bloke was called Sherpa Tensing.

smalls · An ironic term for underpants. Well, ironic in my vati's case: if his underpants were called "massives", that would make more sense.

tig · Apparently Hamburger-a-gogo people call this "tag". I won't ask why because I am full of exhausterosity and also want to go to the piddly-diddly department.

wet · A drippy, useless, nerdy idiot – Lindsay.

whelk boy · A whelk is a horrible shellfish thing that only the truly mad eat. It is slimy and mucus-like. A "whelk boy" is a boy who kisses like a whelk, i.e. a slimy mucussy kisser. Erlack-a-pongoes.

work experience · I include this because I am speaking on behalf of the youth of Britain. He can't speak for himself because he is too stupid. Anyway, whose idea was this? My vati's probably. Teenagers who are innocently filling in time at school, you know, painting their nails, chatting and snoozing, etc. are forced to go to a shop or hospital ward or office or science lab and spend a day there, so that they know what it is like to work. As I have said many times to my mutti, I am far, far too busy to work. And anyway, I know what work is like: it is crap.

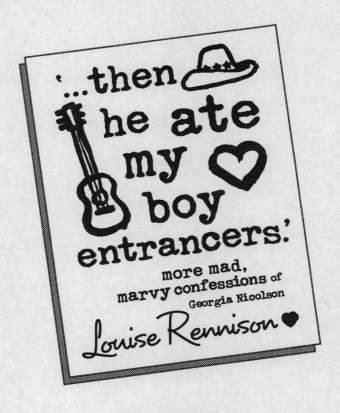

'...then he ate my ♥ boy entrancers.'

more mad, marvy confessions of
Georgia Nicolson

Louise Rennison ♥

P.P.P.P.S.

Turn the page for a sneaky peek
at my next book...

www.georgianicolson.com

Saturday May 7th

Sun shining like a big yellow shining... er warmey thing.

Yessssssssss!

10:05 a.m.

I am quite literally not wandering lonely as a clud, in fact I am treading lightly in the Universe of the Very Nearly Quite Happy.

10:10 a.m.

Something full of miraculosity has happened. My vati, world-renowned fool and paid up member of the Big Twit Club, has for once in his entire life accidentally done something good. We are going to Hamburger-a-gogo land!

Honestly.

And guess who is there already? Besides a lot of people in huge psychedelic shorts and that bloke who is half-chicken half-colonel. I'll tell you who is there – the Sex Meister is there!!

He has gone to visit his olds, leaving me, his new, lurker-free, nearly-girlfriend, back here in Billy Shakespeare land. So he thinks! Imagine how thrilled he will be when I pop up

♥ 291

and say "Howdy!" Or whatever it is they say over there.

Let the overseas snog fest begin!!!

10:15 a.m.

The only fly in the ointmosity of life is that Vati is making us go to some crap clown-car convention.

10:20 a.m.

And Uncle Eddie, the baldest man on the planet, is coming with us too.

10:25 a.m.

Still, with a bit of luck they will both be arrested for indecent exposure when they don their leather motoring trousers.

10:30 a.m.

Filled with the *joie de vivre* that is so much part of my attractive but modest personality, I phoned my bestest pally.

"Jas, it is *miich*, your *sehr guttest* pally, I am calling you *mit wunderbar* news!"

"Oh God. Look, it's only a week till Tom leaves and we were just sorting out my—"

"Jas, I cannot waste time discussing your knicker collection; that is between you and Tom... quite literally... hahahhaha! Do you get it? Do you get it? Knickers... between you and Hunky... do you..."

But, as I should have known from long and tiring experience, it is useless to waste my wit on Jassy. So I cut to the nub and gist.

"I am going to Hamburger-a-gogo land to meet Masimo the Sex Meister."

"No you're not."

"I am."

"How?"

I explained to Jas about the trip and the "Howdy!" business and everything, but as usual she displayed cold waterosity.

"Where is Masimo going to be in Hamburger-a-gogo land?"

"Ahaha!"

"You don't know, do you?"

"Well, not yet, but—"

"He could be anywhere."

"I know, but how big can America be?"

"It's huge."

I laughed. Nothing was going to spoil my peachy mood, let alone some swotty nit-picking.

I said, "Is it as huge as your gym knickers?"

There was silence.

"Jas, come on, be happy for me."

"It's all very well for you, you can just fancy anyone, but it's different with Tom and me. He's off to Kiwi-a-gogo and I will be left here all on my owney."

Oh good grief.

I am going to have to listen to her moaning and rambling on about the twig-collecting years, and snails. Before she could start raving on about molluscs and cuckoo spit, I had a flash of inspirationosity.

"Jas, listen, I have a plan of such geniosity that I have even surprised myself, and might give myself some sort of award."

She didn't even say, "What is it?" There was just silence.

I said, "Aren't you even going to ask me what it is, Jas?"

"It's bound to be stupid."

"Oh cheers, thanks a lot. Well I won't bother you with it, then. Even though it involves you and your happiness and is *très bon* and also vair vair *gut. Au revoir. Bon chance.*"

And I put the phone down. Even Jas cannot spoil my mood. Lalalalalala.

11:00 a.m.
Better start planning my wardrobe for the luuuurve trail. What do the Hamburguese mostly wear? Cowboy hats, I suppose.

11:05 a.m.
And feathers. In recognition of the Native American nation.

11:06 a.m.
I want to make friends with everyone, obviously, but I tell you this – I am not smoking a peace pipe.

11:07 a.m.
Vati will though, sadly, and then probably have an hour-long coughing fit, like he does when he gets drunk and has a Christmas cigar.

Libby will insist on smoking the pipe.

11:10 a.m.

I had forgotten about Libby. How am I going to make sure she doesn't start some international poo incident? From what I hear, the Hamburguese are a bit strict hygiene-wise. It is to be hoped the customs man doesn't glance inside Libby's bag and find her night-time blankin, otherwise we will all be buggered.

Oh, so many things to worry about, I think I will have a little zizz to relax myself and then plan my cosmetic routine for the next week.

11:11 a.m.

Fat chance.

"Gingey!! Gingey, it's meeeeeeee!!! I have just been to the lavatreeeeee!!"

My darling sister has kicked open my bedroom door. Hurrah.

11:13 a.m.

Oh good, and she has her "fwends" with her – scuba-diving Barbie, Charlie Horse, a parsnip and Cross-eyed Gordy.

Our mad kitten, Gordon, is under house arrest because

he has not had the immunisation injections he's supposed to have before he is set loose into the wild jungle world of our street.

I'd like to see the germ hard enough to take him on.

As they all snuggled comfortably into my bed with me, the phone rang downstairs. Vati yelled up, "Georgia, quickly, one of your mates wants to talk rubbish with you for an hour or two on her father's phone."

He has not got the flair of charm, my vati, but on the other hand, what he has got are my tickets to paradise. I must remember that however ludicrous he is, he has bought me a passage to the Luuuurve Machine – Masimo-a-gogo!!!

I shouted down, "Thank you, Papa, I'll be down immediately, and perhaps later I will entertain you with my piano playing."

We haven't got a piano but it's the thought that counts.

11:15 a.m.

It was Jazzy Spazzy... tee hee. I knew she would crumble and want to know my plan.

I said, "So now do you want to know what my plan is?"

297

"If you like."

"No, Jas, you are still not showing enthusiosity. Try harder!"

"I can't."

"Yes you can. Gird your loins and so on, laugh and the world laughs at you. Come on, you do really want to know my plan, especially as it concerns you, my little hairy pally."

"I'm not hairy."

"Have it your own way – just don't go near any circuses."

"Shut up. Go on then, tell me your plan. Although unless you are going to give me the money to go to Kiwi-a-gogo with Tom, I don't—"

"Jas, forget about Hunky, he will be too busy lying around in streams with Robbie, hugging marsupials, to get up to anything. This is about you and me. On the road."

"What road?"

"Ok, this is it: when I go to Hamburger-a-gogo... you come with me! Do you see? Driving across America, you and me; we will be like Thelma and Louise!"

"We're not called Thelma and Louise."

"I know that, I'm just saying we will be LIKE THEM!"

"And we're not American."

"I know that but I—"

"And neither of us can drive."

Oh dear God.

I said, "Jas, your spaceship has arrived. Please get in."

12:00 p.m.

Even Jas has perked up. She wants to come to Hamburger-a-gogo land A LOT. So now all we have to do is get our parents to let us. We have a two-pronged plan.

Prong One is a charm offensive on our muttis and vatis to persuade them to let Jas come to America with me. (And also to give her sqillions of squids for spenderoonies.) We are going to be really nice and sweet and listen to them ramble on about The Beatles and so on before we do the pleading. I've been practising my pleading and you would have to be made of stone not to give me the entire contents of your wallet.

However, if that fails and they say no, we launch Prong Two: Relentless Moaning. You know the kind of thing: "All my other friends are allowed to take a mate on holiday with them. How come I am the ONLY person in the universe who is not allowed to take a mate on holiday? Why is it just ME? Why? Why oh why oh why?"

"Why?"

"It is soooo unfair."

"Why?"

12:10 p.m.

"Why? Why do I never get anything I want?"

12:30 p.m.

"Why?"

Evening

Mutti and Vati are settled down in the front room giggling like loons so, as there is no shouting or breaking of crockery, now is a good time. I'm going in.

Few deep breaths. Ahhhhhhhhhh.

Practise charm. "Good evening. My, what an adorable cardigan you are wearing, Father. And Mother, I have rarely seen you look so slim in those attractive leggings."

Check cheeky-but-lovable grin in mirror.

9:01 p.m.

Blimey that's a bit alarming. I'll ditch the grinning and just let a little smile play around my lips.

9:10 p.m.

Outside the front-room door.

Right, this is it. I've got my old Teletubbies jim-jams on for maximosity on the lovability front.

9:12 p.m.

Mutti and Vati were on the sofa curled round each other. I could clearly see Mum's knickers. Erlack! And the curtains were undrawn; anyone could see in. A fat bloke passing by might think this was a brothel for the porkier gentleman.

I was going to say that, but then I remembered my first prong, so I said, "Good evening, Mother, Father."

Vati said, "How much?" Without even looking at me.

I laughed attractively.

"Oh, Papa, this is not a material matter, it is to do with friendship and love and..."

Mum said, "I don't care how many of your friends have had their navels pierced, you are not."

♡ 301

"But I?"

But she was still rambling on. "Ditto tattoos."

"But I?"

Vati joined in. "And no you cannot have a flat in Paris and a manservant to help with your homework."

Oh how I nearly laughed. Not. I thought about telling Dad that Rosie said he looked like a brothel madam in his flying helmet and leather jacket, but then I remembered my prong.

"You two!!! What are you like? Anyway, all it is really is that, well, you know Jas is all miz because of Tom going to Kiwi-a-gogo... and well, you know she is my pal... and well, it would be nice for me, if... you know... anyway, can she?"

Vati said, "Can she what? Move in? Levitate? What?"

I bit the whatsit.

"Can she come with us to Hamburger-a-gogo land?"

10:00 p.m.

Both of our parents have said yes.

Unbelievable.

Actually, I am not that amazed that Jas's parents said yes, because they are not on the whole entirely mad.

But my parents? Weird.

I'm off to America for a snog fest with the Luuurve God!!!